HOW TO BE COOL

Philip Pullman is a teacher in an Oxford comprehensive. He has written two historical novels and several children's plays. This is his first comic novel.

Philip Pullman

HOW TO BE COOL

Pan Books
London, Sydney and Auckland

First published 1987 by William Heinemann Ltd
This edition published 1988 by Pan Books Ltd,
Cavaye Place, London SW10 9PG
9 8 7 6 5 4 3 2 1
© Philip Pullman 1987
ISBN 0 330 29901 8
Printed and bound in Great Britain by
Richard Clay Ltd, Bungay, Suffolk

For my cool sister Julie

CONTENTS

1

RECRUITING THIS WEEK

Jacob finished combing his hair and adjusting the knots in his trainer laces so that they hung just right, and tucked his pink Italian tennis shirt into his pink jeans, and took his pink belt out of the cupboard. It was a designer belt. He'd designed it. Actually, he'd nicked an old white one of his dad's and felt-tipped it pink, but it had come out all streaky, and on second thoughts . . . He put it back and listened carefully.

His dad was at the allotment, and his mum was at a meeting of the Black Sections Action Policy Sub-Committee, or something, but his sister Louise was bound to be prowling about somewhere. Then there came a blast of sound from her room as she turned the telly on, so he reckoned he was safe. He crept out.

Unfortunately, she had ears like a bat's.

'Where you going?' she yelled.

He sighed, and opened her door. She was slumped in a bean bag guzzling crisps. He was ashamed to have to look at her.

'You ain't watching *Street Noise*? That's terrible,' he said, gazing at the screen.

'Mum said you wasn't to go out till you'd done your homework,' she said.

'I done it. Anyway, I gotta get some exercise, ain't I? People like *die* if they don't get any exercise,' he said, looking meaningfully at the bean bag and the crisps.

But she didn't understand sarcasm. 'I'll tell Mum,'

1

she said, without taking her eyes off the telly, where some blonde girl was bouncing about enthusiastically.

'Get lost,' he said, and shut the door again.

She was like a whale, he thought. Fancy having a sister like that; what with crisps and TV and thinking about sex all day long, she was a wreck already. And she was only fifteen. God help him if he looked like that when he was fifteen.

He got his bike out and rode off to meet the others.

It was ten past seven on a warm Friday evening and the shopping precinct was full of fat men and women and fat kids, and they were all smoking and eating sweets and pushing supermarket trolleys. And wearing track-suits.

Nings and David were waiting at the end by the library, balanced on their bikes with their feet up on the bollards. Nings had blond spiky hair and smart teeth that he'd broken skidding on the ice last winter. They were all jagged and horrible and he'd got a kind of sneer worked out that showed them off brilliantly. David was ordinary-looking, but that was just a disguise. You couldn't really tell how cool he was till he started playing the teachers up; they couldn't take the pressure, any of them, and they just couldn't work out where it was coming from. As for Jacob – when he was five years old, he'd looked exactly like John Conteh, apart from the moustache. But that was years ago. Now he only looked like Jacob: well cool.

He told them about Louise as they rode away.

'What's on *Street Noise* tonight anyway?' said David.

Street Noise was a sort of pop programme, but it was mainly about trends and styles and fashions.

'The graffiti revival,' said Jacob.

'That's been and gone,' said Nings. 'They don't know nothing on that programme. *Street Noise* is well

2

uncool.'

They pedalled slowly through the precinct, taking no notice of the laden families. They didn't notice anything unless it had style – unless it was cool. Then it stood out as if it was spotlit.

They turned a corner near the entrance to the multi-storey car park – and suddenly slammed on their brakes, all three of them together, and just stood there and gasped.

On the brick wall next to the ticket machines, some genius had spray-painted the best graffiti Jacob had ever seen. It was all done in jangly black letters with little tongues of red and orange flame all over it, and the whole word was bathed in a pinky glow that faded magically into the bricks. It was so good he couldn't even read what it said.

'Wow,' said David.

'That's *brilliant*, man,' said Nings reverently.

'I'm going to copy it,' said Jacob. 'I'm going to copy the whole thing before they clean it off. That's the best I've ever seen.'

'They won't ever get that off,' said David. 'That's sunk into the bricks. They'll have to blast it off with a laser.'

'I thought you said the graffiti revival had been and gone,' Jacob asked Nings. 'They must know something on *Street Noise*.'

'They don't know nothing,' Nings said. 'This is different.'

'Well, someone knows,' said Jacob.

He would have liked to sit and look at it for a long time, maybe for minutes even, but they had to get a move on. After a last glance, they cycled on, moving through the crowd like fish through weeds.

They stopped for a moment to look at the display of Adidas shoes in the sports shop. They each had a

3

favourite pair. Jacob used to like the most expensive ones, because it would be pretty cool to have a pair of shoes that cost a hundred pounds, but now he had a new favourite. He couldn't see the label, but they were pink, like his tennis shirt. 'I'm into pink, man,' he'd explained indignantly to his teacher that morning, when the old fool had asked where his school uniform was. Those pink shoes would be really neat.

Oh well.

They took a last look round the well-lit shop to see if they had any new stuff in, and then rode on. It was strange when you thought about it – it was a sports shop all right, but they had hardly any real sports stuff like footballs and that; it was full of clothes for looking cool in.

It was hard to say what *cool* was. You could recognise it straight away, though. You either had it or you didn't. Some people were so cool that they could wear anything and it made no difference, and others were so crummy that they'd never be cool even in hundred-pound shoes and Ferrari sunglasses; but for most people it was just a matter of knowing, like knowing when to start wearing little white towelling socks, or when to stop breakdancing. You had to be good with the timing, though. There was nothing worse than doing something today that had stopped being cool yesterday.

But where did it come from? Who decided to revive graffiti, for instance? Who decided what was going to be cool?

Jacob reckoned that was a job for him, when he left school. He pictured himself in a glow of neon, driving up to a night club in a pink Lamborghini. He'd get out and stand there for a minute, for the photographers, and his clothes would make people *faint*. Then a beautiful girl would get out too and take his arm and there'd be a doorman in a green top hat, and Jacob would throw him

4

the keys of the Lamborghini and give him a hundred-pound note for parking it. 'Oh, Gaf,' the girl would say softly, 'you're so generous!' 'No, baby,' he'd say, 'I'm just cool . . .'

'*Watch what you're doing!*'

A man with three bulging carrier bags was roaring at him. Jacob swerved at the last moment, and frowned at him disapprovingly.

'Give him the heads, lads,' said Nings, and they went into a routine they'd copied from some TV commercial: heads shifting loosely on their necks, up, down, in, out. It needed four of them really, and then it was well funny, like pistons, but Gobbo was having a karate lesson, so it was just the three of them and not so good.

Still, it put the man with the carrier bags in his place.

They swept out of the precinct in the evening sunlight, straight across the road towards the underpass, by the No Cycling sign. There was the usual squad of drunks and junkies draped over the railings or being sick on the pavement, but they were just part of the scenery, like the pathetic hippy twanging a guitar in the middle of the underpass.

But the hippy wasn't there. The underpass was empty except for a kid with a sports bag slung over his shoulder. They raced at him and split apart at the last moment, and he took no notice, which was the cool thing to do, but as they shot past him Jacob saw what was drawn on the piece of paper in the kid's hand, and skidded to a halt.

'You done that graffiti!' he said.

The kid looked up. 'Yeah,' he said.

'Are you gonna do another one here?'

'Yeah. I might.'

'That was *brilliant*, man!'

The kid nodded expressionlessly, and looked back at his paper. He was all dressed in white, and he was dead

5

pale – blond hair, pale blue eyes, dead white skin. He looked as if he spent his whole life underground.

'Hey, Gaf!' David called from the other end. 'You coming or not?'

'You go on,' Jacob shouted. 'I'll catch you up.'

The other two vanished.

'Where are they going?' said the kid.

'To the ice-rink. Skating.'

'Skating?'

The kid's pale eyebrows rose. The ice-rink had been open three or four months, and when they'd set out half an hour before, it had still been cool to go skating. But from the kid's reaction, Jacob knew it wasn't any more.

He was deeply impressed. How did the kid *know*?

The kid opened his bag and spread a square of white cloth on the floor before taking out six spray-cans and standing them in a semi-circle with his bit of paper in the middle.

'Hey, man,' Jacob said, 'how do you – like – you know – I mean, right, how d'you kind of know all that stuff? Like the graffiti and that?'

'It's easy,' said the kid. 'I'm an Agent.'

'An agent? What kind of agent?'

'A Cool Agent. There's got to be Agents, right, to spread what's new, else no-one'd know, would they?'

Jacob shook his head. A Cool Agent!

'Wow,' he said. 'Could I be one?'

The kid picked up a can of paint and shook it hard, so the rattle filled the subway, and then he stood up straight and looked at Jacob. He was the coolest person Jacob had ever seen. He was so cool he was scary.

'It's up to the Board,' he said.

'What kind of board? What you talking about?'

'They're recruiting this week. You might be in time. Just go in there – I'll look after your bike.'

He nodded at a little door in the grey wall. Jacob had never noticed it before. A sign in the middle of it said:

6

'What, I just go in?' Jacob said.

'Yeah. Just go and ask.'

'Wow!'

Jacob dropped his bike and opened the door carefully. There was a dingy corridor inside, with neon lighting and peeling vinyl tiles.

'It doesn't look very cool,' he said suspiciously.

''Course not. That's just the entrance, innit? You don't make big decisions in the entrance. Anyway it's kind of a disguise.'

'Oh, yeah, right,' said Jacob. He'd seen enough James Bond films to understand that the outsides of secret headquarters were always pretty grungy. Further in, there'd be all lasers and remote-control videos and stuff. 'Right,' he said. 'Okay, I'm going in.'

'Okay,' said the kid, and started to spray a big loop of pink on the wall.

Jacob stepped into the corridor. The door closed behind him with a whisper. Jacob, the Agent of Cool! He pictured himself like Clark Kent, all ordinary. Kids would laugh at him in the street; girls would turn their noses up; teachers would think he was trying to work, even. Then night would come, and he'd go out and hit the discos. And the waves of cool would come off him like radiation, and all the kids who'd laughed would be frozen with dread, and the girls would *melt* – 'Oh, Jacob, you're so wonderful!' 'You've got such style, darling!' 'Gaf, honey, dance with me? Please? Mmm?'

'Can I help you?' said a sharp voice.

He blinked. There was a tough-looking woman in the corridor with a pile of papers under her arm, and she was looking at him impatiently.

'Is this the National Cool Board?'

'This is the Research Division, yes. Have you an appointment?'

'I want to be an Agent.'

'Oh,' she said. 'Well, you're in the wrong place. Come along this way and I'll take you to Mr Cashman. He's nearly finished, but he might be able to fit you in.'

'Who's Mr Cashman?'

'The Managing Director. He's interviewing today.'

She led him around a corner. The corridor seemed to go on for miles, with the same dim lights and scruffy vinyl. Finally they got to a smarter-looking part. She opened a door into a little waiting room.

'Wait here, please,' she said.

He went in and sat down, and she disappeared. There was nothing to look at in there, apart from six tatty chairs and an empty coffee table. It wasn't long before he started feeling suspicious again. The National Cool Board? He'd never heard of it. Surely –

Then the door opened, and the woman said, 'Mr Cashman will see you now.'

He followed her out and into the next room along. She showed him in and shut the door behind him.

Jacob looked around. This was more like it. It was a big luxurious place with executive-style lighting and carpets and fittings, and a colossal executive desk. On the desk, next to the two telephones and the intercom, there was even an executive toy – a big pile of ball-bearings stuck to a magnet.

And playing with the executive toy was a really creepy guy. He was wearing a suit, and he had grey hair, and he looked quite normal except for his eyes. They were all flat and cold like the graffiti kid's, and when he blinked, the lower eyelid came up to meet the top one, just like a lizard's. He was watching Jacob without a word.

'Why are you wearing pink?' he said finally.

'I'm into pink, man,' Jacob said. You had to be careful with this guy, he could tell. 'It's cool.'

'You think so?'

Jacob gulped. 'Yeah,' he said. 'It's cooler than this place, anyway. This is well crummy.'

'Really?' said Mr Cashman, shoving his executive toy away and leaning forward to fix Jacob with his weird eyes. 'It may interest you to know, young man, that every trend, style, fashion, and craze which has swept the country in the past forty years was created by the National Cool Board.'

'I don't believe you,' Jacob said. He'd taken a dislike to Mr Cashman. How could an old creep like him be in charge of all the styles? It was ridiculous.

But Mr Cashman just smiled.

'Do you remember the white socks and little black shoes style?' he said.

'Yeah,' said Jacob. 'Course. Why?'

'Let me show you the drawings.'

Mr Cashman got up and opened a drawer in a filing cabinet. He took out a folder and spread it open on the desk. There were drawings of kids' legs in skinny jeans and with all kinds of different socks and shoes: checkered socks and red suede shoes, brown socks and yellow slippers, all kinds of combinations. They all had scribbled comments on them. At the top was a drawing of a pair of legs wearing dark trousers, white socks, and little low-cut black shoes. The comments on this one were: 'This is it!' 'First class!' 'We'll go for this one!'

Jacob was appalled.

'You mean – you made that up? You just invented it?'

'The Research Department developed it, and the Agents promoted it. I understand you want to be an Agent.'

'Well –'

'Would you like to see the Research Department?'

Without waiting for an answer he went to the door and held it open. Doubtfully, Jacob followed.

'They're working round the clock,' Mr Cashman told him. 'There's a big drive on at the moment. A lot of new styles in the pipeline. That's why we're recruiting Agents. What's your name?'

'Jacob.' He thought for a moment. 'Jacob Smith.'

Mr Cashman stopped by a door, and gave him a lizardy blink before opening it.

'The Research Department,' he said.

Jacob looked in with amazement.

The Research Department was a long open room with a row of tables and cubicles and desks in it. There were filing cabinets around the walls and graphs and charts and drawings pinned up everywhere. Seated at the tables and desks were the biggest bunch of creeps Jacob had ever seen, all working away like crazy, talking and writing and drawing and telephoning and things. All the blokes were wearing blazers and ties or sports jackets and cravats, and the girls were wearing tweed skirts and cardigans and pearls, and they all had spots and greasy hair, and they were all saying things like 'What ho, Fiona!' and 'Jolly good, Nigel!'

'Let me introduce you,' said Mr Cashman, putting an icy hand in the middle of Jacob's back and shoving him forward. 'This is Henry, our chief researcher. Henry, this is Jacob. He's going to be an Agent.'

Henry was a stringy-looking guy who'd been staring vacantly at a piece of paper. He stood up and held out his hand to Jacob, who took a nervous step backwards.

'No, hang on, man,' Jacob said to Mr Cashman, 'I changed my mind –'

But Mr Cashman took no notice.

'Show him around, would you, Henry?' he said, and started to go.

10

'Hey! Wait!' Jacob called. 'I don't want to be an Agent!'

Mr Cashman turned and blinked in his sinister way.

'Oh, it's too late now,' he said.

Then he was gone.

'Ha, ha!' said Henry. 'He's a clever chap, Mr Cashman.'

'Yeah, maybe,' said Jacob. 'What's he mean, it's too late?'

'Oh, don't you worry about that. Let me introduce you to the Researchers. I'll let you into one or two secrets now, Jacob. The shape of trends to come! Still, if you're going to be an Agent, you'll have to –'

'I ain't going to be an Agent, man! He got it all wrong!'

'Never mind that,' said Henry cheerfully. 'Come and meet Lizzie. She's our trouser expert. What've you got lined up in the trouser line, Lizzie?'

Lizzie was a gawky kind of girl with a red drippy nose. She smiled up at Jacob in a dopey way that made his flesh creep, and shyly handed him a drawing.

'But that's flares!' he said in horror. 'Flares are *out*! Flares are *dead*!'

'Oh, they're coming back, Jacob,' said Henry. 'We've got them laid on for the New Year. Who knows? You might be the very first Agent to go out into the world and start the flare revival!'

'No – no –'

'Come along and meet Fiona,' Henry said, tugging him forward. 'She's in charge of the under-five cool scene. Tell Jacob what you're working on, Fiona.'

Fiona had big teeth and glasses. She was adjusting something inside a revolting naked doll, and she looked up and gave him a goopy smile.

'Well, oh, hi, Jake,' she said brightly. 'Well, the thing is, we've had lots of different kinds of *realistic* dolls

11

before, you know, I mean they sort of wee-wee and things, but the thing about *real* babies is that a lot of the time they're being sick. So these dolls actually vomit! It's awfully sweet.'

'We're calling them Icky Sickies,' Henry said. 'Would you like to try one?'

'No, no, no –'

'This one's got a bit clogged,' Fiona said. 'I'll have to use a pencil or something.'

She started to jab a pencil down its throat. Jacob felt himself going faint.

'Let me out,' he said. 'Look, I got to go, man –'

'Just come and see this,' Henry said, dragging him a bit further on. 'This is the heart of the future, Jake. This is where it all begins. Remember breakdancing? That started right here, on this bit of floor!'

They were at the end of the room now. Henry pointed at the floor reverently.

'You're nuts,' Jacob said, looking around for an escape route. But Henry had his arm in a firm grip, and went on:

'Yes, this is our Craze Division. Would you like to know what we're working on now? It's going to be the biggest thing for years – it's going to be the coolest craze of the century – tell him, gang!'

And three Researchers swung round in the chairs and spread their hands wide like a chorus line and said:

'FLOWER-ARRANGING!'

Jacob felt his hair stand on end. He made a noise like an Icky Sicky Doll.

'*Yeeuucchhh*! Flower-arranging? You're not serious? You must be crazy –'

'Isn't it wonderful?' Henry said. The Researchers nodded happily and prodded away at some droopy-looking flowers. 'Yes, Jake, it's going to be a classic campaign. The Cool Agents will go out and mix with

12

all the ordinary kids in the schools and discos, and they'll just sort of plant the idea carefully at first, just sort of say Hey, chaps, wouldn't it be cool to do some flower-arranging? Just sort of drop it into the conversation. And –'

'I don't believe it!' said Jacob, struggling. But another one of the Researchers had his other arm now. Henry was looking wild.

'Yes,' he was saying, 'and then they'll do some midnight flower-arrangements in the subways and the multi-storey car parks – like the graffiti thing – and then the Agents will start doing flower-arrangements during lessons, so it gets banned from schools –'

'Let me go! Let me go!'

'The sky's the limit then, Jake. Flower-arranging contests in the clubs and discos – a Sylvester Stallone flower-arranging film – gangs of teenage flower-arrangers cruising the midnight streets –'

Jacob broke free and ran to the door in terror. 'You're all crazy!' he yelled. 'Let me out –'

But when he flung the door open, there was Mr Cashman. Jacob hesitated, and then the Researchers had him again.

'Well, Henry?' said Mr Cashman. 'Have we got an Agent here?'

'Yes, I should say so, Mr Cashman,' said Henry. 'And a jolly good one too. Congratulations, Jake!'

'No!' yelled Jacob, struggling. 'I don't want to be an Agent – no *way*, man! I gotta go – I left my bike in the subway – let go! Put me down! What you *doing*?'

Because half a dozen Researchers had picked him up and begun to carry him off down the corridor and into a room labelled Wardrobe Department. Henry was ticking things off on a clipboard, and Mr Cashman watched approvingly as the Researchers, ignoring Jacob's yells and dodging his feet and fists, took various bits of clothing from the shelves and then pulled Jacob's pink tennis shirt off. Before he knew what had happened, he found himself wearing a home-knitted polo-neck sweater in green wool with a purple pony on the front. Then off came his jeans and his trainers. Henry looked through the clothes on the rack while Jacob contorted himself, tugging the green sweater down to his knees, blazing with indignation and utterly speechless.

'Here we are,' said Henry. 'The knee-length brown Crimplene. Time we tried that out on the street –'

'No! No! No!'

But on they went.

'Now, where did we put the sandals?' Henry said.

'*Sandals?*'

'Oh, yes, everyone'll be wearing sandals in a year or two –'

'Oh, no, you're joking, you don't mean it – no – *please* –'

It was no good. His trainers had vanished, and he found himself wearing grey woolly socks and sandals. He stood there squirming with shame as all the Researchers looked on proudly and Mr Cashman walked round looking him up and down.

'Fine,' he said. 'Well done, Henry.'

'You'll find the skateboard in the underpass,' Henry told Jacob, as they bundled him out of the door and along the passage. 'It's a new –'

'Oh, no, no,' Jacob whimpered, 'not a skateboard, please, man – skateboards are finished – they came back and then they went again – let me have my bike and I'll even wear the sandals –'

'This is a Third Wave skateboard, Jake,' Henry said, opening a door. 'The revival of the revival! Bye-bye, and good luck. Doesn't he look cool, chaps?'

All the Researchers nodded. Jacob felt himself shoved out, and heard the door shut solidly behind him.

Silence.

He peered through his fingers. The graffiti blazed on the wall, and where he'd dropped his bike, there stood a purple skateboard.

He groaned with despair. And then he heard a terrible sound: the air-horn on David's bike. They were coming back! He heard David's voice, and Nings's, and saw them shooting down the tunnel from the other end. He turned away – but it was too late. They screeched to a halt.

'Gaf!' they said.

And then, 'Where you been?'

And then, 'Where's your bike?'

And then, 'What's that – a skateboard?'

And then, 'What're you *wearing*?'

'Shut up!' said Jacob. 'You just don't know what's cool.'

But it didn't sound very convincing, even to him. They hooted with laughter.

'Shut *up*, you *crumbs*!' he yelled. 'I tell you, this is *cool*! I been inside the National Cool Board! I *know*, man!'

'The what?' said David, in between hoots. 'The what did he say?'

'The National Cool Board!' said Nings, and clutched his sides with hysterical laughter.

'I *did*, I tell you! It's just in there – look –'

Jacob turned in fury to show them the door. But it had vanished. There was nothing there but a smooth grey wall.

'Hey!' he said. 'They've hidden the door. What a bunch of creeps – it was there, I swear it was! The National Cool Board!'

He flapped across the underpass in case it had been on the other side, and David pointed to his feet.

'Look, Nings!' he said. 'Fairy-boots!'

They clutched each other, helpless with laughter.

15

Jacob was about to throw himself at them in a passion, but heard footsteps. There were *people* coming. They might *see* him. He scuttled around behind David and Nings and stood there trembling till the subway was empty again.

'What's going on, man?' said Nings.

'Yeah, what's it all about?' said David.

'It's the most terrible thing that ever happened,' he said. 'It's a catastrophe.' He looked carefully to left and right, but there was no-one coming. Nings and David were worried now; they could see he meant it. They listened, awestruck, as he began to explain. 'You know all the styles, right, and all the trends and that – well, I just found out where they come from ...'

He began to explain as they moved away.

Meanwhile, somewhere in the Cool Board, a little blinking light began to move across a video screen. The screen showed a map of the city, and the video operator made a note of where the light was going. Mr Cashman stood back and nodded.

'Good,' he said. 'Another Agent on his way. Keep a sharp eye on this one – he'll need a lot of supervision.'

The operator said 'Right you are, Mr Cashman. We'll watch him night and day.'

'I hope you will,' said Mr Cashman, and went back to his office.

Half an hour and several detours later, the boys got to the old canal. While David and Nings kept watch, Jacob climbed the rickety bridge and bunged the skateboard into the water.

'Right,' he said. 'They're not making a fool of *me*, and that's a fact.'

But he still had to get home. It was nightmarish. The worst bit was when he was creeping along below the level of the hedge so as not to be seen by the little girls in the house next door. He was so anxious about them that he didn't see Louise and her friend Amy staring at him from the front door. Not till they started shrieking with laughter, anyway.

'Shut up!' he said, but he wasn't in any position to swop insults, so he bombed around to the kitchen and went in that way.

When the dog saw him, it howled with fear and ran under the table.

'Oh, not you, too, Mouldy,' he said in despair.

He grabbed a handful of swiss roll from the cake tin and shoved it at the trembling hound, and then shot upstairs to get out of the terrible clothes. It was like a nightmare. His pink tennis shirt – his pink jeans – his bike – the *shame* –

Still, at least he'd got rid of the skateboard.

Actually, that was the best thing he could have done. As soon as it hit the water, the little light on the video screen went out. The Shakuhachi KM3600 Creepisneek microbug attached to the skateboard had been tested in all kinds of extreme climatic conditions, but it had never had to cope with the sheer concentration of poisonous gunge in the old canal, and it gave up at once.

The video operator blinked, and tapped the screen, and jiggled the switches, and turned the contrast up and down. Then he reached for the phone and dialled Mr Cashman's number. This wasn't going to be easy ...

2

IF HE CAN UNDERSTAND IT . . .

Next day, Jacob's classroom was full of meaningful, creative activity. The previous teacher had had a nervous breakdown, and her replacement hadn't got the hang of things yet, so she was still trying to make the kids work.

Well, they were certainly busy.

It was a General Studies period. On Jacob's private timetable, though, it was marked with the word DOSS. That didn't mean it was easy. You couldn't just sit there – you had to look as if you were doing something, and that took effort.

There were several kinds of doss going on.

Five boys, including Jacob's mate Gobbo, were doing a survey. They said they were finding out how many fish fingers the class ate in a week. All they had to do was go round with bits of paper, and as long as they made random marks on them from time to time, they could go anywhere and talk to anyone. It was great.

Another good scheme was to cut pictures out of magazines and stick them in your book. That was extra good because you could leave bits of paper and glue all over the place and make the teacher well eggy. The trouble was that they only let you do it if you were thick, usually, and in any case there weren't many magazines left in Jacob's classroom. So there were only two girls doing this.

The best doss of all was to do a bit of drama. You just

got a group of about six of you and you could scrap, make a noise, do what you liked. This teacher had got a bit wary of drama, though, ever since Nings had smashed the blackboard by trying to take it out in the corridor to be a giant video screen for a space cruiser, so she only let the quiet kids do it now.

But Jacob and Nings and David were doing posters. The topic this term was Advertising. They'd done Advertising the previous year in English and the year before that in Humanities, so they knew exactly what to do: a big poster from each of them advertising something, and they were safe for six weeks.

So everything was normal.

And then Jacob had an idea.

This was a new sensation for him. Normally he never had ideas at school. He blamed the uniform. 'I mean how can I think if I'm covered in green?' he'd say indignantly. 'It's not natural.' The teachers expected him to work whether he was thinking or not, though. He couldn't understand them.

But this idea was wicked. It was:

Set up another organization and beat the National Cool Board at their own game.

Or:

Get them before they get you.

Because they were definitely out to get him. He'd had a creepy feeling ever since he'd left the Cool Board, and when he'd bunged the skateboard in the canal, he'd felt as if Mr Cashman himself might appear out of the murky water, all dripping with weeds and dead cats and stuff, like one of the Swamp Zombies in a video Jacob had seen last month.

And even his sister Louise was getting suspicious. She'd looked up over her cornflakes this morning and blinked at him, and he could have sworn her bottom eyelid came up to meet the top one, just like Mr

Cashman's. There was no doubt about it, she was weird.

When the bell went, he didn't let the others play football as they usually did. Instead he dragged them round to where it was a bit quieter, by the Science room. Gobbo came too. He was trying to karate a stick, and he set it up between two stones on the wall while Jacob told them his idea.

'That's well wicked,' said Gobbo when he'd heard it. He karate'd the stick and it flew into the air unbroken. 'I'll be an Agent!'

'We all got to be Agents,' said Jacob. 'We got to have hundreds of 'em.'

'Where you going to get 'em from?' said David. He and Nings had come to believe what Jacob had told them about the Cool Board; they'd had to, in the end, what with the sandals and everything. 'I mean ...'

He pointed at the other kids in the playground. They were all running round playing tig or showing their stickers to each other or doing terrible things like that.

Gobbo karate'd the stick again. This time it fell off the wall.

'Yeah, well ...' said Jacob. 'We'll just have to train 'em, that's all.'

'You can't train someone to be cool,' said Nings. 'That's like training 'em to have red hair. You're either cool or you're not.'

'Well, *they* do it,' said Jacob. 'Anyway, I bet we could. Anyway, we got to.'

'But how?' said Nings, as Gobbo's stick flew up in the air again.

'It's easy,' said Jacob. 'We just recruit hundreds of 'em and get 'em all doing cool things. Except they'll be our cool and not the Cool Board's cool. Then we send 'em out and they get to work, and then the Cool Board goes out of business.'

Gobbo karate'd the stick for the fourth time, and it finally broke.

'Look at that, lads!' he said. 'I done it!'

'Yeah, brilliant,' said Nings. 'Why not use a saw? It'd be a lot quicker.'

'It'd be quicker with a trained woodworm,' said David.

'Right,' said Jacob absently. He was thinking of a name for the organization. Cool Incorporated? Cool Unlimited? The Cool Council?

They came back to it during French. Gobbo didn't do French, on account of being thick at Maths, but the others were pretty ace at Maths, so they had to do French. It was a bit dangerous, because the French guy was a maniac. He just would not speak English.

This morning they were pretending to sell plastic vegetables to each other. When the teacher wasn't looking, they worked out a plan of action.

'Qu'est-ce que c'est this horrible ugly purple thing?' said Nings.

'It's an aubergine,' David told him. 'Don't you know nothing?'

'Oh, right. We could call it the School for Cool.'

'No-one's going to join anything called a school, are they?' said David. 'Watch out. Combien est-ce que le cauliflower?'

'Choufleur! Choufleur!' shrieked the teacher from across the room.

'Oui, oui. Le shloofloof c'est combien?'

'Je ne sais pas,' said Jacob. It was the only French he felt sure about. 'It's gotta have *cool* in it, though . . .'

The tables in the room were crowded together, because the place was jammed with trolleys and empty wine bottles and cheese packets and French bingo games, and so the kids on the next table heard what they were talking about. One of them was a girl called Deirdre. She had short scruffy blonde hair and eyes as light as the graffiti kid's, only sort of alive instead of flat, and she had all the girls in the class right under her control.

'How To Be Cool,' she said.

'Eh?' said Jacob. 'What you talking about?'

'If you want to get people interested,' she said, 'you ought to put that on a poster. All big kind of jangly writing. And underneath it just a phone number. No-one'll be able to resist that.'

'That's brilliant, man!' said David.

Jacob wasn't sure. And who'd asked her anyway? But then he thought of all the followers she had. Maybe they ought to have her in on it.

'Yeah,' he said. 'I reckon that's okay. Watch out ...'

'Est-ce que les oofs est combien?' said Nings.

'Oofs is eggs, you wally,' said Jacob. 'I ain't got any oofs. Here,' he said to Deirdre, 'd'you want to be a director?'

Deirdre looked at him coolly. Well, she was quite cool, he thought.

'Who's the boss?' she said.

'Me, of course,' said Jacob. 'This is going to be *big*. It's going to be gigantic, right? It's going to be a mega-doss.'

'All right,' she said. 'I'll join. Mind out ...'

The French teacher was stalking them with a little French frown on his forehead. They went back to their vegetables.

'C'est combien?' David was saying. 'Quel terrible prix. Look at the state of this pomme ...'

That was the poster they finally came up with. Jacob thought of the bit about the frontiers of style, and he reckoned it was so brilliant it had to go in. But they kept Deirdre's headline.

HOW TO BE COOL

AGENTS NEEDED FOR A HIGHLY **DANGEROUS** MISSION ON THE FRONTIERS OF **STYLE**

DUDES PREFERRED, BUT TRAINING GIVEN TO CREEPS ETC. CONTACT **GAF** 3P

They tried it out on Gobbo first. If he could understand it, David said, then anyone could. He stared at it for a whole minute. They could tell he was really reading it, because his lips were moving.

'Yeah,' he said finally. 'Smart. That's well wicked.'

'What's it mean then?' said Deirdre.

'I dunno,' he said. 'It's about dudes and that. It's pretty smart.'

'Oh, fair enough,' said Nings. 'Bung it up then, Gaf.'

'We'll need a whole load of them,' said David. 'I reckon we ought to do four each at least.'

'And put 'em up in the town as well, not just in the school,' said Deirdre. 'In the subway, for a start.'

That made Jacob's blood run cold. He hadn't told her about the trouble he'd had with the Cool Board – well, not all of it. Some things were too shameful for mixed company, and sandals were one of them. Actually, he was thinking of advertising on the telly. Sticking bits of felt-tipped paper up around the place was all very well, but he had bigger plans than that.

Still, they had to start somewhere. The classroom went dead quiet as the five of them bent over their pieces of paper. The sun shone in and the felt-tips squeaked industriously and the National Cool Board had no idea what was going to hit it.

3

INSIDE THE COOL BOARD

Meanwhile, Henry the chief researcher was in big trouble.

As soon as the light on Jacob's video-trace had gone out, Mr Cashman had put out a general alarm. They'd recovered the drowned skateboard, but there was no sign of Jacob, so Mr Cashman did what every experienced manager does in a crisis, and looked for someone else to take the blame.

He sat at his executive-style Bolo-wood veneer desk and rolled his ball-bearings about on the leather-look blotter, while Henry trembled on the carpet in front of him.

'You did *what*?' Mr Cashman said.

'Well, I told him about ... about the Icky Sickies. And things. But –'

'What things?'

'Well, flower-arranging. But –'

'Flower-arranging? You mean to say you told him about *flower-arranging*? Do you realise what this means?'

'But I thought he was going to be an Agent! I mean, you said!'

'Enough,' snarled Mr Cashman, pressing a button on the glittering console in front of him.

Immediately a door slid open and in drifted Sylvianne, Mr Cashman's beautiful secretary. She was wearing a gold velvet dress and her hair was all piled up high in great scoops and curls, carefully dyed in three different colours for a natural look. She was a nice girl, but she was as thick as two planks.

'You called, Mr Cashman?' she whispered softly, one hand up on the side of the door frame in the way they'd taught her in the Cool Board Training Centre.

'Yes. Take this ex-chief researcher to the side entrance and get rid of him.'

Henry gasped. 'Not – not the outside world! Please, Mr Cashman! Anything but that!'

Mr Cashman looked at him with his cold lizardy eyes, and Sylvianne pressed one manicured hand to her bosom to express shock and amazement.

'Very well,' said Mr Cashman after a long pause. 'One last chance, and I mean last. This boy has got to be found, you understand? Found and ... dealt with.'

Sylvianne gulped, but Henry practically wept with gratitude.

'Oh, yes, Mr Cashman! Certainly! My word! I'll catch the little rotter all right! I'll make him sorry! You wait and see!'

'Results, Henry,' snarled Mr Cashman. 'Action.'

'Yes sir! Right away!' Henry gibbered, and he actually bowed, he was so terrified.

Sylvianne, melting with admiration for Mr Cashman, led him away. Mr Cashman pressed the button to close the conference-centre-style sliding door, and leaned back in his executive chair to close his creepy eyes in thought.

Jacob had only seen a small part of the National Cool Board. It was a huge organization, with dozens of departments as well as the Research Division. There was the Training Centre, where Sylvianne had learned to pose in doorways and carry trays of Martini and do all the other things cool secretaries had to do; there was the Personnel Section, where they deal with everything from recruitment to pension schemes for ex-Agents who were living as fifty-year-old Teddy Boys in Clacton or forty-year-old hippies in a wigwam in Wales; there was the Archives Division, there was Manufacturing, there was Accounts – it was a colossal enterprise.

And then Jacob had come along . . .

Mr Cashman opened his eyes and pressed a button on the arm of his chair, and a little intercom unit slid up out of the top of the desk.

'Yes, Mr Cashman?' said Sylvianne's squeaky voice.

'Halve the Icky Sicky budget,' he said. 'And put flower-arranging on hold.'

'Icky Sicky budget halved, flower-arranging on hold,' she trilled. 'Anything else, Mr Cashman?'

'Yes,' he said. 'Get me the head of the Detrendifying Squad. This is an emergency.'

Every so often an unofficial trend would break out. Naturally, the Cool Board couldn't allow that, so they had a Detrendifying Squad to deal with it, headed by a hard nut called Alex. Alex had stamped out all kinds of things in his time, from a rash of yo-yos in Plymouth to a nasty outbreak of classical music in Scunthorpe.

'This is a difficult one, Alex,' said Mr Cashman when Alex was finally sitting in the office. 'I've got a feeling we're up against real trouble, but I don't know where it's going to break out.'

He explained what had happened. Alex's little eyes were like stones.

'Careless,' he said. 'I'm gonna need extra bodies for this, Mr Cashman. Plus a twenty-four hour command centre with full surveillance faculties. We got our hands full at the moment. They just started *stamp-collecting* in Wolverhampton.' An expression of disgust passed over his hard little face. 'If I go after this Jacob geezer, I'm gonna have to let that go, Mr Cashman.'

'Then let it go,' said Mr Cashman. 'Beside the damage this boy could do, stamp-collecting is peanuts. Oh – a clue,' he added, as Alex rose to go. 'Look out for pink.'

Before long, all the resources of the Cool Board were being cranked around to focus on Jacob. They set up an Operations Room, with a huge table where girls pushed little flags about with long poles while the men stood around telling them what to do.

Mr Cashman put Lizzie, the trouser expert, in charge of the Research Division. She was dead keen. She worked about twenty hours a day, making lists of everything Jacob had seen while he was there, and re-designing it. The flares had to go, of course. It was a hard decision, but she was pretty tough, and she slung all the drawings in the Gobble-O-Trash document shredder without a second thought. The other research assistants didn't know what had hit them. There was no 'Super, Nigel!' or 'Ya, Fiona!' any more; this was the real thing.

Finally Mr Cashman did something that had never been done before: he cancelled all leave for the Cool Board employees. No-one could have their weeks in Spain or fortnights on a Greek island with Club Different until Jacob had been found.

Mr Cashman hardly had time even for his favourite preoccupation, which was wondering whether or not to change the name of the National Cool Board. All the other big organizations were doing that, but he couldn't make up his mind whether it was a good idea or not. To settle it, he decided to ask the dimmest person he knew.

'Sylvianne,' he said, 'we're thinking of changing the name of the Cool Board. What do you think of *British Cool*?'

Sylvianne put her finger to her chin and tilted her head on one side, as the Training Centre had taught her to do when she had to think.

'I think it sounds *schoopid*,' she said finally.

'Good,' he said. 'So do I. We'll stay as we are for the time being.'

The reason for all this panic was simple. The Government was planning to de-nationalize the Cool Board and sell it off to private investors. Any snarl-ups could have serious consequences for the big banks, for the City of London, for the entire economy of the country, especially now that North Sea oil was running out. Without knowing it, Jacob had stumbled into a very big game indeed.

4

THE COOLOMETER

'Right,' said Jacob. 'Thank you, yeah, we got your number, right, we'll be in touch.'

The latest applicant turned to go, and Jacob scrumpled up his form and dropped it with all the others under the table.

'Wow,' said Deirdre.

'How many more?' said Nings. 'I don't think I can stand this, man, I think I'm going nuts ...'

'There's three more,' said David. 'You want the next one?'

'Yeah,' said Jacob. 'Bung 'em in. They can't be any worse than what we seen already.'

It was the lunch hour. They'd found an empty classroom, and conned a note out of the English teacher by pretending they were working on a bit of drama. He was a soft touch for anything with drama in it, and armed with his note they could fend off the old Gorgons who stomped around the place doing dinner supervision. This was the third recruitment session they'd had, and they hadn't found anyone decent yet.

'Right,' said Jacob as the latest candidate crept in. 'Name?'

'Jane,' came a tiny voice. The kid it came from was tiny too. Jacob thought, she must be about five years old. What are they doing letting kids like this into school?

'Right,' he said. 'Walk across the room and look

cool.'

'I dunno how to,' she whispered.

'Show her, Gaf,' said David.

'No! If I show her then we won't know what she can do, will we? Now come on,' he said to the kid, 'are you going to walk across the room and look cool or not?'

In reply she burst into tears and ran out.

'What'd I *do*?' said Jacob, as the others all looked at him reproachfully. 'If she wants to be an Agent, she's gonna have to be cool, ain't she? It *says* dangerous on the poster, doesn't it? I mean this takes *nerve*, right? These are professionals, these guys we're up against. You don't seem to *realise*!'

'How many we seen so far?' said Deirdre.

'Seventy-two,' said Nings.

'How many we taken on?'

'None.'

'All the cool kids around think it's a joke,' said David. 'We're getting all the rejects and the wimps and that. How long till the bell?'

'Ten minutes,' said Deirdre. 'There's two more out there, right?'

'Yeah. One of 'em's well weird.'

'Well, we'll see him last,' said Jacob. 'Send in the other one.'

David opened the door and a kid from their class came in.

'Name,' said Jacob.

'Ah, come on, you know me, Gaf,' said the kid.

'D'you wanna be an Agent or not?' said Jacob angrily. He was in no mood to mess about. 'Name.'

'Prakash Bhandari,' said the kid. 'And you better spell it right and all.'

He was a skinny little guy with sharp quick eyes, and about the coolest one they'd seen all day. Still, Jacob was determined to make him do the tests.

31

'Okay, stand over there and look cool,' he said, while Nings wrote down Prakash's name.

'No, listen, I ain't come here to be an Agent. I got something to show you, right. It's a Coolometer.'

Silence.

'Get lost,' said David uncertainly. 'Stop wasting our time. Coolometers my left leg.'

'Your loss, mate,' said Prakash cheerfully. 'I been working on this for a year already. I can always find a market for it somewhere else.'

'No, hang on,' said Jacob hurriedly, thinking of the Cool Board. 'What is it, then?'

'It's a Coolometer. It measures cool. You want to talk about it?'

'What d'you mean, it measures cool?' said Nings. 'How can you measure cool?'

'With a Coolometer,' said Prakash.

'What you talking about?' said David. 'You gone nuts.'

'No, let him explain,' said Deirdre.

'Right, what it does,' said Prakash, pulling out a chair and sitting down, 'it's electronic, right, and it's sort of like radar, only instead of electro-magnetic waves, it picks up cool waves.'

The others looked at him, and then at Jacob. This was tricky, Jacob thought. What do I say now?

'Yeah,' he said. 'Cool waves. Right. What then?'

'Well, you can measure 'em. Or even get a bearing on where they're coming from. Or –'

'Hang on,' said Deirdre. 'I never heard of cool waves.'

'Course not,' said Prakash. 'No-one has. I reckon I'm the first person to discover 'em. See, there's only a few fundamental forces in the universe. Electro-magnetism's one, and gravity's another, and I reckon cool waves are, too. There could be a Nobel Prize in this.

32

Here,' he said, breaking off and leaning a little closer, 'who's that geezer outside?'

'Why?' said Jacob.

'He looks a right nut.'

'Never mind him. We'll see him in a minute. Where's this Coolometer then?'

'At home. It's a bit big, right.'

'How big?'

'Sort of wheelbarrow size. I'm trying to miniaturize it, but I ain't got the finance.'

'Yeah, right,' Jacob said. Cool waves! he thought. Huh! 'Okay, when can we see it then?'

'It's round my place. In our shed. You can come round after school.'

'Righto,' said Nings. 'Now get lost. We only got three minutes till the bell.'

Prakash went out.

'Cool waves,' said Deirdre. 'Wow.'

'Shut up,' said David. 'He might have something, you never know. Shall I show the last bloke in?'

'Yeah, go on,' said Jacob. He was thinking: if we could get a fix on the Cool Board, we could keep track of them. That's not a bad idea at all.

The last candidate came in, and David shut the door.

'Er – hello, Jake,' said a voice.

Jacob looked up, and felt his eyes pop.

It was Henry, the chief researcher.

Jacob jumped up in a panic, but then he got hold of himself and sat down again.

'What you doing here?' he said, frowning sternly.

The others were staring, open-mouthed. Henry was in disguise: he was wearing overalls and carrying a toolbag so as to look as if he was doing some job around the school, and he'd got lacquer on his hair to make it all stand up, and he had a pair of sunglasses pushed up on his forehead.

'What d'you think of the disguise, Jake?' he said. 'Pretty streetwise, eh?'

'Who's this?' said Deirdre.

'It's a bloke from the Cool Board,' said Jacob. His mind was racing. 'What d'you want?' he said. 'You can't come here. This is private.'

'I've come to be a mole,' said Henry. 'No, listen, Jake, this is desperately serious. Mr Cashman's got a big alert on. I'm supposed to be looking for you.'

An alert! Jacob imagined his face on a *Wanted* poster, with bristles on his chin and a mean hat low over his eyes, like Clint Eastwood. He'd be an outlaw! There'd be a price on his head! He felt the others looking at him with awe.

'Yeah,' he said. 'Wow.'

Then the bell went. Henry jumped like a streetwise antelope.

'You better move, man,' Jacob told him. 'Meet us down the Rec at four o'clock. Go on, quick ...'

'The Wreck?'

'Yeah, the Recreation Ground – now get lost, go on, you can't stay here –'

They were shoving him out, and he was protesting, and a crowd of little weenies was swirling around them trying to get into the classroom, and Jacob was thinking: Wow! It's real! I'm an *outlaw*!

He was so impressed that he spent the whole afternoon working. Peace reigned in the classroom. Everything was quiet. The class did more work that afternoon than in the whole of the previous month.

At four o'clock they found Henry lurking on a seat by the swings. He still had his toolbag and his sunglasses, but he'd ditched the overalls. He looked dead nervous.

'Right,' said Jacob. 'Now you better deliver, or else.'

'Yes! Yes! Anything!' said Henry. 'What d'you want to know?'

'Everything,' said Jacob.

Henry glanced at Deirdre and Gobbo and David and Nings. They all stood round him menacingly. Nings gave him *the teeth*, his well-known snarl, and Henry trembled.

'Right,' he said, gulping, and began.

Ten minutes later they knew as much about the Cool Board as he did. He told them about the Detrendifying Squad, about the Government's privatisation plans, about production forecasts for the Icky Sickies, everything. When he'd finished they sat for a long time without saying anything – for nearly fifteen seconds, in fact.

'Wow,' said Jacob finally. 'How did you find us?'

'I saw your poster,' said Henry. 'And if *I* found it –'

'The Detrendifying Squad!' said Jacob. 'Oh no! Gobbo – Nings – get on your bikes and bomb round taking down all the posters – quick! Every single one!'

They shot away, scattering gravel, and Jacob turned back to Henry.

'Right,' he said. 'If they want a fight, they can have one. We've only been messing about up till now. But this is *war*!'

'Gosh,' said Henry. 'I say.'

'And we got a secret weapon, and all,' Jacob went on. He'd have told Henry about the Coolometer if Deirdre hadn't interrupted.

'What's he want, though?' she said, meaning Henry.

'Yeah, what *are* you playing at?' said David.

'He's a mole!' said Jacob.

'Why?' said David.

Jacob didn't know. They all looked at Henry.

'What are you playing at?' Jacob asked him sternly.

Henry wriggled a bit. 'Well, you see,' he said, 'I think

Mr Cashman's got it in for me. I think he was going to sack me even before this came up. And *I* want to be the boss! I'm jolly ambitious, you know, Jake. I'd make a super Managing Director. But while he's there, my career's just going into a downward spiral towards the plughole of life.'

'Oh,' said Jacob. 'Well, I tell you what. You can come in with us, right. But only if you pay the price.'

'Anything!'

Henry was practically clapping his hands with gratitude.

'My bike,' said Jacob. 'And my pink T-shirt and jeans, and my trainers. They nicked 'em, and I want 'em back.'

'But – but –'

'That's the price,' Jacob told him firmly. 'You get them back, and we'll look after you when we take over the Cool Board. Otherwise . . .'

He put on a sinister look. Deirdre spoilt it a bit by laughing at him, but Henry didn't notice.

'I guess I've got no choice,' he said despondently. 'Right, Jake. I'll do my best.'

'This is where we'll meet, then,' Jacob said. 'After school, right. Every day. If you can't make it then leave a message stuck under the bench with bubble-gum.'

'If he can't get here then how can he leave a message?' said Deirdre.

'That's for him to figure out,' said Jacob, who couldn't work it out either. 'Now clear off and do some spying, man. We got business to see to.'

When they got to Prakash's house, they found his dad outside with his head under the bonnet of his car.

'You going in to see Prakash?' he said. 'You tell him I want my damn shed back. I've got tools standing in the garden going rusty and lying about the house getting under people's feet and driving my mother mad, poor old lady, she came down the stairs yesterday and fell right over the lawn-mower, she's still talking about it now. The sooner he gets his crazy rubbish out the better. I think the boy's insane, they'll have to lock him up soon, it won't be too soon for me, I promise you that. Where is he? Oh, he's down there now. Go down the garden. Don't go anywhere near my mother or you'll have to listen all about the lawn-mower, and she's excitable enough as it is. You tell him from me, I want my damn shed back ...'

Well, Prakash certainly seemed to have his dad organised, Jacob thought. And Mr Bhandari was massive, too – about the size of Mount Everest.

They made their way through the garden and found the door of the shed open, with a weird humming noise coming from inside. Just as they got there, there was a bang and a shower of sparks, and Prakash leapt out of the door, followed by a smell of burning.

'Wotcher,' he said when he'd picked himself up. 'Just trying it off the mains. I ran this cable down last night, right, but I reckon the transformer's on the blink. You want to have a go?'

'What've I got to do?' said Jacob, peering suspiciously in through the door.

'You just come flying out covered in sparks,' said David. 'Nothing to it.'

'You do it then,' said Deirdre.

'No,' he said. 'I'll let Gobbo have my go.'

'It ain't dangerous,' said Prakash. 'I better put it back on the batteries just for the demonstration. Give us a hand, Gaf. We'll fetch it out on the path.'

Prakash's dad was a telephone engineer, and the shed was packed with all kinds of smart tools and coils of wire and transformers and batteries and things. At least, that was what it looked like. They all turned out to be attached to the Coolometer, as Jacob found when he tried to shift it. With him and Prakash shoving from inside and the other two hauling from the doorway, they finally got it on to the path and stood back to have a look at it. And just then, Gobbo and Nings arrived.

'We got 'em all!' said Gobbo.

'There was some blokes in the subway looking at the one down there,' said Nings. 'They says to us, "D'you know anything about this, then?"'

'The Detrendifying Squad!' Jacob said, appalled. 'What'd you say?'

'It was brilliant, man!' Gobbo chortled. 'You oughter heard Nings! He says, "It's all under control. Special orders of Mr Cashman. You carry on, lads." And they went!'

'It's mainly 'cause I gave 'em *the teeth*,' said Nings modestly. 'They was real hard-looking nuts and all.'

'What's he talking about?' said Prakash. 'You all gone mad?'

'Never mind,' said Jacob. 'You show us how this thing works, and then we'll tell you.'

They all looked at the Coolometer. Jacob had never seen such a pile of junk in all his life. There was an old telly in the middle of it, and a couple of car batteries, and a complicated thing made out of a load of metal coathangers, and switches and dials and wires and handles and bits of string and rubber bands and springs, and a bottle half-full of dirty water with a copper tube sticking out of it.

'What's that for?' said Jacob, pointing to the bottle.

'That's the radiator,' Prakash explained. 'It gets well hot when it's working. Stand back, then. I'm not sure how it's going to react in the open air. The cool waves are a bit unpredictable ...'

They took a step back as Prakash fiddled with the coathangers and adjusted a couple of knobs. Then he switched it on, and after a flash and a spark or two and a bit of smoke, it started to hum.

'What's it doing?' Deirdre said.

'Just picking 'em up,' Prakash said. 'Watch the screen, right. That's where they show up first.'

Gobbo already was, but then he'd watch anything. There was all kinds of stuff going on: cartoons, a weatherman, adverts, a newsreader, all flickering past each other as if the set had gone crazy. Then they all vanished suddenly and a weird pattern appeared instead. And something else happened: the coathangers were starting to jiggle.

'You're doing that!' Jacob said.

'No I ain't!' Prakash said. 'That's the aerial. Watch out – don't touch it –'

As Jacob brought his hand closer, the aerial started jumping up and down like a mad chicken. Suddenly there was a loud *twang* and a clatter as all the coathangers fell apart, and a rubber band holding them together flew through the air and hit Nings right on the nose.

He yelled with surprise and anger. Everything got a bit confused then. Prakash was scrambling for his coathangers, and David was laughing, and Deirdre was telling Jacob off for breaking the aerial, and Jacob was holding Nings away from Prakash. The only peaceful one was Gobbo. He was watching the telly, where an old *Magic Roundabout* had suddenly appeared out of some time-warp.

'It wasn't my fault!' Jacob said, when things had calmed down. 'Anyone'd think I'd booted it or something. I never touched it.'

'There was just too much cool going in,' said Prakash, wrapping the coathangers round each other again. 'It's never had all that much to cope with before.'

'Oh,' said Jacob, pleased. 'Yeah, that's what it was. All the waves I'm giving off.'

Nings was asking David to look at his nose, and David was saying yeah, it was horrible. Prakash stuck the aerial back in. The *Magic Roundabout* vanished, and Gobbo gave a little sigh of disappointment.

'Right,' said Prakash, 'we'll try it again, okay, only this time do what I say. We gotta shield the cool, right. Gaf, put your school uniform on.'

Jacob had dropped his crummy school sweatshirt back on the path somewhere. 'What?' he said. 'I ain't wearing that, man! That's *green!*'

'Do what he says,' Deirdre told him. 'You're less cool with it on, right?'

'Yeah, dead right.'

'Well, the waves'll be less strong, won't they?'

'Oh. Yeah. I suppose you're right. Well, that'll prove it, anyway,' Jacob said, and dragged the sweatshirt over his head.

They all crowded round to watch as Prakash turned it on. He twiddled some knobs and adjusted the aerial, and presently it began to jiggle. Nings got behind Deirdre in case it shot him again, and the others peered over Prakash's shoulder as he tapped a dial.

'What's that doing there?' Gobbo said. 'It's a speedometer!'

'That's off my brother's motor bike. The only other dial I could find was marked in pounds per square inch, right, but the linkage was too complicated.'

The aerial was jiggling away quietly, and there was about ten miles an hour worth of cool coming into the Coolometer.

'Right, Gaf, go round the front,' Prakash told him. 'Not too close – that's it. Stand still.'

The needle went up to twenty miles an hour.

'Now walk back a bit – that's it – hang on – right. It's about ten miles an hour now. Okay, take the sweatshirt off.'

Jacob did, and straightaway the aerial jiggled a bit harder, and the needle went up to twenty-five.

'Hey! It works!' said David.

'What's happening?' Jacob called. 'What's the rate, man? What'm I scoring?'

'Twenty-five,' Deirdre said.

'What's it go up to?'

'A hundred,' said Prakash. 'But that's only this dial, right. I dunno what the maximum would be. It might be a thousand.'

'Absolute cool,' said David. 'Let's have a go. I bet I'm cooler than Gaf.'

He went round in front, and the needle wobbled up further. Jacob peered, frowning.

'Thirty,' said Nings. 'Lemme try. I'll give it *the teeth*.'

He stood in front of the aerial and snarled. It jumped suddenly and he leapt backwards in alarm.

'What'd I get? What'd I get?' he said.

'Fifty for *the teeth*, then it went back to five when you jumped,' Prakash told him.

'Yeah, it's not cool to be nervous of a bunch of coathangers,' Deirdre said. 'You can't fool the Cool-ometer.'

'What's my rate then?' Jacob said, shoving the other two out of the way and posing like a bodybuilder in front of the aerial.

'Thirty-five,' said Prakash.

'Is that all?' He struck another pose, and the needle trembled a bit higher. 'I thought I was cooler'n that. I know what it is! It's me school trousers. They're shielding the waves.'

'Take 'em off, then,' said David helpfully.

'Mind my grandma,' said Prakash nervously. 'She'll have a heart attack ...'

Gobbo wandered around the front to see if the *Magic Roundabout* had come back, and suddenly Prakash and

Deirdre both gasped together.

'What? What?' said Jacob.

'Look at this!' Deirdre said.

Jacob, David, and Nings crowded round to look at the dial. The needle was pressing so hard against the hundred-miles-an-hour stop that it was bending. Then, as they watched, it snapped, and the stump went whizzing round about fourteen times before trembling to a halt.

'It's Gobbo,' Nings whispered.

They stared at him in awe. He was gazing placidly at the screen, with a dopey smile on his face.

'Mr Ultimate,' said David. 'The coolest guy in the world!'

'Incredible,' said Nings.

'That's it!' said Jacob. 'We can do it now, lads! We got everything we need to beat the Cool Board!'

'For crying out loud, what's this Cool Board? What's it all about?' said Prakash.

'Oh yeah!' said Jacob. 'We never told you. Okay, you better join us, right. We'll need the Coolometer, and that's a fact. Anyway, it's like this ...'

He explained, and Nings and David went on testing their cool while Deirdre gazed thoughtfully at Gobbo.

Next door, old Mrs Jackson's telly was playing up. She'd been peacefully watching *Grange Hill* when all of a sudden it went FLITSKRITSKAPEEWEEE and she found herself watching the news from Turkey.

'Cor, look at that, Bill,' she said to her budgie. 'We got the Welsh programme again. There'll be *SuperTed* in a minute, I expect. That's your favourite.'

In the house on the other side, Mrs Fuller was trying out her new microwave oven. All her kids were sitting round the table waiting for the Baked Bean and Avocado Crumble, which had taken all of six minutes to cook, and her husband was washing his hands in the sink.

Then the timer clicked its way round to zero, but instead of going *ding*, the microwave spoke.

'*Get off! It's my turn*,' it said, and then in a different voice, '*That's only fourteen miles an hour. That's not cool.*' Then the first voice said, '*Well how can anyone be cool when their nose is all swelling up like an aubergine?*'

The Fuller family stared at the microwave oven, silent and terrified.

In fact all up and down the street strange things were happening as the cool waves, amplified by one of the coathangers, spread out and hit the local electronics. But no-one had a worse time than Prakash's poor Grandma. She was just edging her way past the lawn-mower in the hall, when it switched itself on and chased her half-way up the stairs. Then it changed its mind and sang Country and Western songs to her until Jacob and the others had had enough of the Coolometer and switched it off. Everything went back to normal then.

'Okay?' Jacob said. 'We don't recruit anyone else, right. It's too dangerous. We'll borrow your Dad's wheelbarrow and take the Coolometer to my place. Tomorrow we'll take it down town and hunt the Cool Board!'

5

MIDNIGHT MANOEUVRES

It was midnight in the Cool Board. The only people in the place were the Ops Room crew and the security guards. Everything was quiet.

The security guards didn't have a great deal to do. In the old days, they used to make cups of tea and read the *Daily Mirror* all night long. They had an old Alsatian called Mandy, and they'd walk her up and down every hour or so, for the exercise. But the guards they had now came from a private firm called Beet-U-Up Security Systems, and they all had moustaches and crash helmets and truncheons, and they got drinks out of the coffee machine and read the *Sun*.

As the digital wall-clocks flicked their way round to midnight, one of these guards was creeping along a corridor near the Research Department. This guard was a bit unusual, because he had bandy legs instead of short fat ones, and he looked nervous.

He stopped outside a door, looked both ways down the corridor, and fumbled at a bunch of keys till he found the one he wanted. A moment later he was inside the door.

Then he had a shock, because the light was on, and there was a girl sitting on the floor with a notebook.

She looked up and said 'Henry!'

He leapt as if someone had fired an ice-cube up his trouser leg.

'I – I – who are you?' he gulped.

'Sandra, from the Ops Room,' she said. 'It *is* Henry, isn't it?'

'Well ... Actually, it is,' he said, taking off his crash helmet. 'But what are you doing here?'

'It's my tea break,' she explained. 'It's nice and quiet in here. I come here to write poetry.'

She was a droopy-looking girl with dark hair. Henry felt a bit silly standing there in his false moustache, so he thought he'd better explain.

'Can you keep a secret?' he said.

'Oh, yes!'

'Well – I don't work here any more. I'm a double agent!'

'No! Really? But what are you doing in the store-room?'

'I've come to liberate a bike. And some clothes. This is a desperate mission, Sandra. My whole career's on the line. You promise you won't give me away?'

'Gosh! You bet! But who are you working for now?'

'Ah, I can't tell you that. But ...' He looked around carefully. 'But how would you feel about spying for me? Sort of letting me know what's going on? I can't make too many trips like this. The Board's days are numbered, Sandra. It's going to fall! And you can help me bring about a better future ...'

He took her hand and looked at her passionately. She was quite pretty, really, with the light behind her, and if you blinked a bit.

She was thinking something similar about him. He hadn't got his false moustache on quite straight, and he had a spot on his nose, but if you didn't actually look at him he was quite good-looking, in an unusual way.

'Yes,' she whispered.

'Oh, Sandra!'

'Oh, Henry!'

They didn't quite have the nerve to kiss each other,

but they certainly thought about it. Then Henry got all stern and commanding, and told her a phone number where she could contact him. She wrote it in her poetry book while he fetched Jacob's bike and stuffed the clothes under his jacket.

She opened the door and kept watch while he wheeled the bike out and disappeared into the night. He'd never felt so cool in his entire life.

Meanwhile, Alex had called a midnight meeting of the Detrendifying Squad. They held it in the cafeteria of the Travellers' Tum All-Nite Carvery and Motel. Alex liked having meetings there, because he could scowl at all the other customers and look hard. They were mostly too zonked from driving along the motorway to notice him, in fact, but he didn't know that.

'Right,' he said, when they were all sitting on the little perches they had for chairs. He snapped open his individual portion of Plastikreem and let it drip into his coffee while the other Detrendifiers waited respectfully. 'What we got so far?'

'I seen two girls with white lipstick today,' one of them said. 'In just over five minutes. And they was both wearing ski pants.'

'You know the rules,' Alex said. 'Two is a tendency. Three is a trend. Anyway, we're looking for a geezer. If you got nothing better than that, go back out and keep looking.'

'Sorry, Alex,' said the Detrendifier.

'I got summat,' another one said. 'Three cars, right, and they all had like zebra-skin seat covers.'

'This geezer's too young to drive a car,' said Alex. 'Nice try, though. We'll do summat about that when this job's over. Anything else?'

'I found this, Alex,' said another. 'It was on a bus stop.'

He handed over a rolled-up piece of paper. Alex

unrolled it, and sat up at once.

'What's this? "How To Be Cool? Agents needed ..."'

It was one of Jacob's posters that Gobbo and Nings had overlooked. As Alex read it, another Detrendifier peered over his shoulder.

'Here – I seen one of them! Down in a subway! There was a kid taking it down,' he said.

'Didn't you speak to him?' said Alex.

'Well, 'course I did.'

'And?' Alex could be dead menacing sometimes.

'He said it was okay,' the Detrendifier mumbled, ''cause like Mr Cashman knew about it, and he was sorting it out ...'

'Bird-brain!' Alex snarled. 'Don't you realise what this means?'

'Sorry ...'

'There's a phone number on there, Alex,' said someone else.

'I can see, I can see!'

He hadn't actually noticed it, but he did now. It was Jacob's number. They'd put it on all the posters they'd stuck up in the town.

Alex folded the paper and put it in his pocket.

'Promising,' he said. 'Distinctly promising. But it was a stroke of luck. I'm not having my squad relying on luck. I want hard graft. I want you out there on the streets with your eyes peeled. Now go back out there and get on with it.'

The squad left. Alex sat there for a few minutes and finished his coffee. On the way out he passed a table where four men were sitting, and saw that they each had an identical striped tie on. A regimental reunion? Or were they trying to start a trend? He gave them a hard little scowl, just in case.

At about the same time, Jacob was lying awake in bed, thinking.

They'd got the Coolometer; they'd got Henry moling for them; they'd discovered Gobbo's incredible gift; everything should have been fine.

All the same, Jacob was worried.

What was bothering him was the fact that pretty soon he'd have to start thinking up some trends, or some cool things to do, or something. He'd never had to do that before. He was dead smart at picking up all the cool that came from outside, like hip hop and bodybuilding and stuff. There was no-one quicker at that in the whole school. But he'd never actually made anything up.

(And to think that all the time it was being made up by those creeps in the Research Department! It brought him out in chilly little shivers just to think of it. It was going to be a *crusade*, this fight).

But they'd never beat the Cool Board unless they could come up with some brilliant ideas. And who had they got to think of them?

Gobbo was no good, in spite of his sensational rating on the Coolometer. He didn't have an idea in his head. He wouldn't know what an idea was if you sent him one in a box with a label on it, because he probably wouldn't know how to read the label. So he was out.

Prakash was a genius, fair enough. But not at inventing cool. He could measure it, sure, and Jacob betted the Cool Board itself hadn't thought of a Coolometer, but he'd never be able to generate it, not in a hundred years.

Nings . . . Well, he'd had a couple of good ideas in his time. Working out how to do *the teeth* was pretty smart, and he could ride his bike backwards, which nobody else could do. But you wouldn't beat the Cool Board by riding bikes backwards at them, and you couldn't do *the teeth* unless you cracked them the right way first. Somehow Jacob couldn't see hundreds of kids hurling themselves face down on the ice in the hope of being able to snarl like Nings.

David, now . . . He might be able to. David's cool was a bit of a mystery. He'd got it, but you couldn't see it, though you knew it was there. Prakash had been going on about high-energy cool fields, or something – they'd discovered that David's cool rating got higher the further he was from the Coolometer. Weird. But if he didn't know what he was doing, then he wouldn't be able to do it to order. Maybe. Difficult.

Which left Deirdre. She was the weirdest of all. She could stand in front of the Coolometer and do nothing and make the needle (after Prakash had repaired it) show anything from nought to sixty miles an hour just by thinking about it. Was girls' cool different from boys' cool? Was it unisex? Did even the Cool Board know what they were doing when they made it up? Could Deirdre invent some cool stuff?

Jacob didn't know, and he couldn't sleep. He was discovering the loneliness of command.

6

THERE'S NOTHING TO IT

As it happened, he had a brilliant idea the very next morning, at breakfast. It was all because of Louise, really. She looked out of the kitchen window and said 'Dad!'

Their dad looked terrible in the mornings. He had a shameful old dressing-gown and his eyes were all bloodshot and the little bit of hair he had left was sticking out in all directions. He wasn't really conscious at breakfast, and he could only speak in grunts.

'Uhh?' he said, as his trembling hand brought the coffee to his lips.

'Jacob's left the shed door open, look,' said Louise.

Jacob wasn't going to let her get away with that. 'How d'you know it was me?' he said. 'It might have been you. You're always doing things and blaming it on me. I bet you came down in the middle of the night and sneaked out to open it on purpose so's you could accuse me now. I bet —'

'Enough!' That was his mum. 'You've got a voice like a circular saw, boy. For goodness' sake let's have some civilized behaviour at the breakfast table. I've given up expecting civilized standards from your father, the poor man's catatonic or something until eleven o'clock, but I will not give up the struggle to civilize my children. Louise, you brought the subject up. Go and shut the shed door. Jacob, go and get the paper. I heard it come through the door. It gets here later and later every day . . .'

They both started to argue, but she just looked at them and they shut up.

Jacob dragged the bundle of papers out of the letter box. It was fat today; as well as his mum's paper there was Louise's magazine. It was called *New Modes* and it had all the latest stuff about pop groups and fashion and clothes and so on. She went nuts if she missed it.

Well, she'd miss it this week all right. He stuffed it into his school bag, which he'd accidentally let fall from the landing just as she was going downstairs earlier on. Right! So much for *New Modes*.

Then *pow*! An idea hit him right in the back of the neck. He snatched the magazine out of his bag again and opened it up.

He was right. In tiny print at the foot of the second page it said *New Modes is a National Cool Board production*. The idea rose up, all big and shimmering and wobbly, like a bubble; and he shoved the magazine back in his bag and took the paper to the kitchen.

His mum took it from him just as Louise came back from the garden.

'It *was* him,' she said, with her little eyes glinting. 'He's making drugs in there!'

'Oh, drugs,' said his dad. 'Uhh.'

'Drugs?' his mum was suspicious at once. 'What's this?'

'I dunno what she's talking about,' Jacob said. 'You know she's mad. You don't want to listen to her. It only encourages her.'

'What is this about drugs?' his mum said sharply. 'Richard, are you listening?'

'Uhh,' said his dad.

'He's got a weird machine in the shed, and he's bound to be using it to make drugs,' Louise said, taking the last piece of toast.

'That's my piece,' Jacob said. 'Put it back. You're the size of a rhinoceros already.'

'Get lost,' she said, slapping butter on it, and their mum slammed the paper down on the table.

'What is all this about?' she said. Jacob felt sorry for her clients; she was an educational psychologist, but the way she went on, you'd think she was the chief interrogator for the secret police of the planet Zargon. She was as dangerous as a cross between Mr Cashman and Tina Turner.

'I'll swear he's making drugs,' Louise said again, with her mouth full of toast. 'It's just the sort of thing he would do.'

'Do not speak with your mouth full!' their mum snapped.

Then their dad blinked so you could practically hear his eyelids creak, and said, 'He couldn't be.'

'Why not?' said Louise, swallowing.

'Because he's not clever enough. No brain.'

'Oh, thanks, Dad,' Jacob said bitterly.

'And you're deluded,' his dad said to Louise. 'I've said it before. It's monosodium glutamate and artificial colourings and polyphosphates in the food and it's lead in the petrol and above all it's that goddam television. You're completely insane. Raving. Hallucinations, frothing at the mouth –'

'That's just toast,' their mum said. 'Shut your mouth when you eat, girl.'

'– weird machines in the shed,' their dad went on. 'You'll be hearing voices in your head next and forgetting where you've put things. Then you'll start thinking you're a pineapple. Then they'll come and take you away. And then we can all have some peace.'

'Finished?' said their mum. 'I think I prefer you catatonic, on the whole. Now look at the time. Go on, hurry up, get to school.'

'Where's my *New Modes*?' said Louise. 'I bet he's nicked it ...'

'See?' said their dad. 'What'd I say? Voices in the head next.'

'Get out! Go on! Go!'

The first lesson that day was Science, so Jacob could settle down and look at *New Modes* in peace. The Science teacher was a Scottish nutcase who went rock-climbing, or pretended to, and sometimes he'd come clanking into school with climbing boots on and pitons hanging off him as if he'd just got back from the Alps. It was pitiful, really, especially since he reckoned that all the girls fancied him.

Anyway, he was dead easy to distract. Jacob told Deirdre what to do, and she organised a bunch of girls to play up to him, and while MacNab spent the lesson smirking and flirting with them, Jacob and David and Nings worked out an ace plan.

Then the bell went, and they shot out and cornered Gobbo by the bike sheds.

'No *way*, man! Not in a hundred years!' Gobbo said. 'You won't *never* get me doing that, no way!'

'You won't even know it's happening,' Jacob told him.

'It doesn't hurt,' said Nings. 'There's nothing to it.'

'It'll only last a couple of minutes,' said David. 'You won't hardly feel it.'

'But why *me*?'

'Because you're the coolest, right?' Jacob said. He was beginning to lose his patience. 'Anyone'd think it was going to be *painful*. Anyone'd think we were asking for blood or something.'

'The *shame*,' moaned Gobbo, seeing there was no escape. He unthinkingly karate'd the side of the bike shed in his despair, and hurt his hand. 'A *male model* . . .'

He was practically whimpering with panic.

'Well, so what?' Jacob demanded. 'We got to sort the Cool Board out, right? And if we get *our* style and *our* cool all over *their* magazine, then we'll win the first round, won't we? And it's gotta be you 'cause you got the highest rating of all time on the Coolometer. There's no-one else who could do it, man. You're unique. Anyway there's hundreds of guys who have their pictures taken and stuck in adverts. Every day. There's nothing to it.'

'Anyway,' said David, 'if you don't want to do it, there's no problem.'

'Why?' said Gobbo, hopefully.

''Cause we'll just thump you. Okay?'

On Saturday morning they were all set. Deirdre got a camera from her dad, who was a photographer, and who'd been trying to get her interested in photography for years. He even gave her a roll of film. They mounted the Coolometer on Ning's old truck, which he'd used for bombing down the hills on his estate when he was a kid, and they caught Gobbo again and Nings and David marched him down town, where they were going to take the photographs.

He made a scene about that, too. He wanted to have them taken somewhere hidden away out of sight, but Jacob overruled it.

'Locations, man,' he said. 'Ain't you heard of locations? Anyway, look –' He shoved *New Modes* at him. 'This is the way to do it.'

All the pictures in *New Modes* had tough-looking ginks lounging about next to dustbins, looking moody, or sprawled across old motorbikes wearing T-shirts, and they all had bulging muscles and neat haircuts. They were supposed to be advertising things, but you could never tell what.

'Can't we do it different?' said Gobbo, but no-one took any notice.

It wasn't easy manoeuvring the Coolometer through the crowds, especially since Ning's truck couldn't turn right. The steering problem had occurred one afternoon when David had been bombing down the hill into the car park; he'd missed the turn and gone flying into the fence. It had been really impressive to watch, but the truck would never turn right afterwards, so they had to give it up.

As well as the Coolometer, the truck was carrying a load of different clothes and things for Gobbo to wear. Deirdre had got her mate Julie to be in charge of all that. Julie had fancied Gobbo for some time, so she was well pleased to be brought in. She had it all worked out, hairstyles, clothes, shoes, the lot. Gobbo kept making little whimpering sounds, and twitching slightly, but Nings and David kept a firm hold, and he didn't get away.

The sun was shining, and all the punks and the drunks and the junkies draped over the benches in Memorial Square were looking pretty clean, for once. Jacob reckoned it was as good a place as any. They trundled the Coolometer up the steps and on to the grass, and Gobbo turned pale.

'Not here,' he said. 'Please!'

They took no notice. Prakash connected up the Coolometer, Jacob and Deirdre and Julie worked out the first sequence of shots, and then Nings and David held Gobbo down while Julie did his hair. They soon had a pretty interested audience. Since the punks had nothing to do but hang about and sneer at people, they were keen to come and see what was going on, and there were plenty of kids drifting about, as well as normal shoppers. Before they'd even started there was a crowd four or five deep all round them, making helpful comments.

'Right,' said Jacob, taking command. 'Give us a bit of space. Let's have that rubbish bin over here – that's it. I saw a dog here a minute ago – where is it? Fetch him over here, Nings. Is Gobbo ready? Check his rating first. We got to do this properly, right. Okay. Stand back, ladies and gentlemen, let the mighty Gobbo get to the Coolometer.'

The coathangers were jiggling away gently and Prakash was at the controls. He'd fitted a new gauge, a rev counter this time, off his brother-in-law's old MG. It gave a cool rating in revolutions per minute instead of miles per hour, but it went up in thousands instead of tens, which was the only way it could cope with the sheer power of Gobbo's cool waves.

The crowd stood aside respectfully as Julie led Gobbo up to the Coolometer. She'd sprayed his hair so that one side of it stood up in a great wild wave and the other side lay flat on his skull, and he was wearing huge old green corduroy trousers that Jacob had nicked from his dad's wardrobe and a thermal vest that Julie had dyed black. It had come out a streaky sort of grey, but at least it looked different from anything the Cool Board would come up with, Jacob reckoned.

There was a murmur of interest in the crowd as Gobbo stood in front of the Coolometer and Prakash took the reading.

'Two thousand five hundred r.p.m,' he said. 'That's nice. That's okay.'

David wrote it down, and Jacob set up the first picture, using the dog that Nings had found. He stuck it in the rubbish bin so its paws were resting on the edge and its head was looking out, well suspicious, and he told Gobbo to go over and look at it, spreading his hands and opening his mouth so as to look amazed. It looked brilliant, but the dog kept jumping out, so the first three shots Deirdre took were of Gobbo looking amazed at an empty bin.

Finally they got it right, and Julie took Gobbo off to get ready for the next shot. Jacob took the opportunity of making a speech.

'Ladies and gentlemen,' he began, 'you may be asking yourselves, "What is going on? Who are these strange talented people? What is this unusual jiggling machine?" Well, right, I shall tell you. We have no secrets from the public. Our organisation is called *How To Be Cool*. This is the world's first and only Coolometer, invented by the guy over there, Prakash. It measures the cool waves, recently discovered by him, right, and after our photo session, we can give you all a cool rating on the machine for a small fee. The subject of our photo session today, shortly to be featured in a world-famous national magazine, and now being sorted out by my lovely assistant Julie, is the mighty Gobbo, Mr Ultimate, the coolest guy in the world. And here he comes for picture number two.'

The crowd all stood aside and watched. The punks cheered, and even the drunks shouted something or other. This time Julie had stuck a seaside Kiss-Me-Quick hat on the flat side of his head, and given him a sailor's jersey that she'd found in her attic. He still had the corduroy trousers on, because there was nowhere for him to change, but he had tattoos drawn all up his left arm. When he heard the applause he brightened up and gave them a grin.

'Okay,' said Jacob, 'now for this sequence, right, the great Gobbo is going to arm-wrestle this teddy bear.'

It was David's teddy bear. It had done all kinds of things in its time, but it had never arm-wrestled a sailor in front of a crowd of punks before. David was a bit worried in case Gobbo wrestled its arm off. Still, it seemed to go all right, and both contestants got a cheer, and Deirdre got her picture.

In fact everything was going fine. The crowd liked Jacob's speeches, and the sun kept shining, and Gobbo began to relax, getting cooler and cooler all the time. And Deirdre was taking some smart pictures. Jacob was well pleased.

However . . .

In the Ops Room at the Cool Board, there was a crisis going on. All the monitoring equipment had suddenly gone haywire; there were signals coming in from Cyprus and Russia and Cheltenham, and a lot of gibberish that no-one could work out at all, but which was actually a phone-in programme from the planet Blebgugbex, on the fringe of the universe.

In fact, the cool waves were causing chaos. All over the city traffic lights went crazy, police messages were being broadcast over all the food processors in Electricity showrooms, TV sets were flinging themselves to the floor and sucking at the carpet like vacuum cleaners, and a man who rang up for a taxi found himself speaking to a Blebgugbexian gardening expert, who couldn't understand him, either.

The guy in charge of the Ops Room that morning was Squadron-Leader Simmonds. 'Don't panic!' he was yelling, as the lights flashed on and off and the girls with the long poles got their flags all tangled up. 'Don't panic, chaps! Not to worry!'

Most of the radio operators couldn't take the pressure, and had given up. But one of them fought his way through the chaos and shook Squadron-Leader Simmonds's shoulder.

'Sir!' he said. 'I don't know how to explain this – but we seem to be picking up an entirely new form of energy –'

The door flew open, and in came Mr Cashman,

closely followed by Sylvianne.

'What the devil's going on?' he snapped. 'Squadron-Leader! What's happening?'

Squadron-Leader Simmonds pulled himself together and saluted.

'Entirely new form of energy, sir,' he said. 'Buckets of it. Machines can't cope. Not to worry unduly –'

Just then a jet of oxtail soup from the coffee machine caught him right in the ear and he fell to the floor, still saluting.

Mr Cashman looked around at the devastation.

'What was that man gibbering about?' he snarled at the radio operator. 'New form of energy?'

'There's interference on all our frequencies, Mr Cashman – it's putting out colossal amounts of energy – I've never seen wave-patterns like this before! I don't know if the equipment can take it!'

'Try. You track it down. Get a bearing on it, and we'll stamp it out. Sylvianne!'

'Oh, Mr Cashman!' she squeaked, fluttering her hands.

'Alert the Detrendifying Squad. I want them on the streets at once. Then get back here.'

'Mr Cashman! Mr Cashman!' yelled another of the radio operators. 'I think I've got it –'

Mr Cashman stepped over the Squadron-Leader and went to peer over the operator's shoulder.

'Well?'

'Signals are strongest in this sector here, Mr Cashman – they seem to be coming from somewhere in the neighbourhood of Memorial Square ...'

'Right!' said Mr Cashman, and a frosty little smile of satisfaction appeared on his face. 'We've got him now. He won't get away this time.'

Meanwhile, the photographic session was coming to an end. Or rather, Deirdre was running out of film. They certainly weren't running out of ideas. Even the punks and the drunks came up with some, which they tested on the Coolometer first to make sure they were okay, and they put some of the punks in a couple of pictures, too.

As for the Coolometer, it was jiggling away like crazy. Jacob was busy hustling money from people who wanted to test their cool rating; Nings had to give *the teeth* to one or two kids who were getting too nosy; Gobbo was signing autographs, or at least making a sort of mark on the page; an ice-cream van and a couple of buskers had arrived to work the crowd; Julie was being interviewed by a local radio reporter; and Prakash was talking electronics with two or three computer freaks in anoraks.

It was such a colossal success that no-one noticed the Ford Transit drawing up at the edge of the square, and the hard-looking nuts getting out of it, and the extra-hard-looking nut speaking into a car phone. It was Alex. The Detrendifying Squad had arrived.

Louise was in town that morning, hanging about with her friend Amy. They went there every Saturday to look at boys. They'd been up and down the market and had a hamburger and a couple of coffees and some chips and a Mars bar already, and it was only eleven o'clock and they were bored. They were each plugged in to their portable stereos, so they had to shout to hear each other. They spent a bit of time outside the sports shop, talking extra loud to try and attract the attention of the hunk who was arranging the window, but he took no notice, so they got fed up and decided they didn't fancy him anyway.

It was about then that Jacob and the others started the Coolometer going in Memorial Square, and the amplified cool waves spread out and hit all the electronics in the city.

They soon reached Louise's Wallicorder. Instead of *The Golden Greats of Andrew Ridgley* she found herself listening to a weird conversation. Two blokes were trying to talk to each other through a stream of interference. She banged the Wallicorder, but it made no difference, and she suddenly remembered what her dad had said about hearing voices in her head. He'd said something about forgetting where she'd put things, too ... Maybe Jacob hadn't nicked *New Modes*. Maybe she *was* going bonkers.

She started to sweat a bit, and listened to the voices more closely.

'*Alex? Alex – is that you?*'

'*There's a lot of interference, Mr Cashman – can you hear me?*'

'*Yes – I can hear you – now listen to me: get the squad and go to Memorial Square. Got that?*'

'*Memorial Square – right. What then?*'

'*Something's going on, Alex. I don't know what it is, but I think our friend's involved. Young Jacob. I want you to get down there at once and ... rescue him.*'

Louise jumped. Jacob? This wasn't voices in her head – this was his drugs gang planning something. She pressed the earphones closer.

'*What's that, Mr Cashman?*'

'*I said find Jacob and take him to ... A place of safety. I can't say more over an open line. Have you got a large vehicle? There might be a group of them.*'

'*We got the Transit, Mr Cashman. Right you are – we'll rescue him all right. He'll be in a place of safety before you can SKREEEEEEET – ZIP ZIP ZIP ZIP ZOW WOW WOW WOW ...*'

Louise unplugged herself. Was she hearing things? Or wasn't she? There was only one way to tell.

'Give us this,' she said, and snatched Amy's earphones off. 'What you got in here?'

'Madonna,' said Amy, bursting a bubble.

Louise put Amy's earphones on.

'*Hello?*' she heard. '*Montrose Taxis? Anyone there speak English? Hello? Taxis? I want a taxi! Please! Parlez-vous anglais? Je suis at the station – hello! Montrose Taxis?*'

So Amy's stereo was playing up as well, only Amy hadn't noticed. A grim little smile came to Louise's face. So Jacob was in trouble, eh? It must be a rival gang. Or even the police. And *his* gang was belting off there to help him ...

'I'll sort *him* out,' she said to herself, and grabbing Amy, she dragged her as fast as she could to Memorial Square.

They arrived just before the Detrendifying Squad, and Louise was able to tell Amy what was going on.

'It's my brother, right,' she said. 'He's been making drugs in the shed, and he's in dead trouble now, and they're sending someone to rescue him.'

'Who?' Amy couldn't understand.

'I dunno – his gang or summat – I heard 'em speaking on the radio. But I'm gonna fool 'em.'

'Why?'

''Cause he's always getting *me* in trouble. Anyway if he's making drugs he deserves to get done. I ain't going to help him. Look! There they are ...'

She remembered the voices: '*We got the Transit, Mr Cashman* ...' Well, there was a Transit van drawing up now, and the Detrendifiers getting out of it looked just as she thought a gang ought to look.

She ran up to Alex as he was about to move the Squad into the crowd, and grabbed his arm.

'Here,' she said, breathless, 'you're looking for Jacob, ain't you?'

He frowned. 'How do you know?'

'He ain't here - he's just gone! Message from Mr Cashman,' she said, remembering a name from the radio. 'If you want to find him, you better get after him quick.'

'Where's he gone, then?'

'I dunno – he got in this big American car, right,' said Louise, making it up wildly, 'with some blokes with dark glasses, and they went off that way – about three minutes ago! It looked like he was being *kidnapped*!'

Alex's little eyes couldn't open very wide, but they opened as wide as they could. Kidnapped? What was this, then? Another group? Or someone helping Jacob to escape from the Squad?

'How d'you know him, anyway?' he said suspiciously.

'He's my brother, innee?'

'Oh. And you reckon we –'

'You're going to rescue him, ain't yer? And take him to a place of safety? Well, you better get a move on, else you'll lose him.'

Alex was totally confused. He thought he'd better test her.

'What colour was this American car, then?' he said.

'Pink,' she said. It was the first thing that came into her head.

Alex remembered what Mr Cashman had told him about Jacob: *Look out for pink*. This was it, all right! They had him now!

'Back in the van, lads,' he called, and as they all piled in he said 'Ta, love. What's your name, then?'

'Louise.'

'Right, Louise. We'll – er – we'll look after your brother all right. Ta-ta.'

He jumped in and slammed the door, and the van shot off towards the by-pass.

'I didn't fancy *him*,' said Amy. 'He was like a weasel.'

63

She burst a big pink bubble. Louise dragged her away; she didn't want to be around when they arrested Jacob.

The cool waves weren't being broadcast anymore, because they'd turned off the Coolometer, so everyone was happy. Mr Cashman was pleased, because the radio channels had gone clear and it sounded as if Alex was on to it at last; Louise was pleased, because she reckoned she'd fooled the people who were going to rescue Jacob, so he'd get into dead trouble; Jacob was pleased, because they'd made four pounds fifty out of giving cool ratings to the crowd, and got some brilliant pictures. In fact, everyone was pleased.

It was a good day.

7

COPY. SPIEL. WORDS.

Henry didn't think so, though. They met him later at the Rec, and told him what to do, and he got nearly as panicky as Gobbo had.

But Deirdre had worked out how to deal with that.

'You can do it, honest,' she said. 'We couldn't go to a place like that, could we? I mean we're just not as sophisticated as you.'

'Oh,' said Henry. You could see him thinking about it. 'Well, perhaps not. But all the same –'

'I mean it's going to take real sort of *nerve* to go to the editor of *New Modes* and tell him that this was the latest stuff from the Cool Board and he'd got to print it. I don't think anyone in the world could do it better than you, Henry. Honest.'

'Ah,' Henry said. 'Mmm, yes. I see what you mean. But –'

'I mean you've got a sort of masterfulness, kind of thing –'

'Like James Bond,' put in Julie.

The boys were watching, amazed, but it seemed to be working. Henry was standing a bit taller, and squaring his shoulders and narrowing his eyes to look tough. He was imagining how impressed Sandra would be when she heard about it.

'Okay,' he said. 'Leave it to me. Same time, same place?'

'Oh, Henry,' said Deirdre, handing him the film.

'That's wonderful . . .'

He gave her a sophisticated little smile, unfolded his sunglasses with a sophisticated flick of his hand, and stuck them on his nose.

'Ciao,' he said.

'Ta-ra,' said Julie. 'Thanks, Henry . . .'

Both the girls gave him dopey smiles as he sauntered away. He was being so sophisticated that he didn't see the concrete around the swings, but they pretended not to notice when he fell over it.

'Blimey,' said Nings. 'What a twit.'

'Shut up,' said Gobbo. 'He's all right, old Henry.'

'Hmm,' said Jacob. 'We'll see. If he gets the pictures in *New Modes*, then he'll be all right.'

Henry and Sandra went for a walk on Sunday, and she read some of her poetry to him. He reckoned it was brilliant. On the way back they held hands. He was so excited by this that he told her what he was going to do, and she practically fainted with admiration.

'You will be careful, won't you?' she said.

'It's got to be done,' said Henry, all brave and masterful.

Actually he didn't feel brave and masterful at all. He felt terrified, and when he got on the train on Monday morning he wished he'd never heard of Jacob, or the Cool Board, come to that.

He got to the *New Modes* office at twelve o'clock. The building it was in was all made of glass and bronze and filled with executive-style rubber plants and Bolo-wood contemporary fittings, and the girl at the reception desk was so glamorous that she made him feel like an advert for spots.

'Er – can I see the editor of *New Modes*, please?' he said. 'Miss.'

'Tenth floor,' she said. 'Sir.'

She looked him up and down, and he crept away to

66

the lift. On the way up he kept saying to himself, 'I am cool. I am sophisticated. I am tough and masterful. I am cool. I am sophisticated,' and so on. It didn't seem to make much difference.

The editor's office, when he finally got there, was a scruffy little place full of cigarette smoke and used paper cups. Henry had rehearsed a whole speech about how this film was very important, the latest thing from the Cool Board, major feature, front cover, etc, etc. But he didn't get the chance to make it, because the editor, a miserable-looking middle-aged man with braces, came out and said 'You from the Cool Board?'

'Er – yes,' said Henry. 'Actually, this is –'

'Let's have it,' said the editor. 'What they want this time?'

'A big feature,' said Henry. 'Special treatment. Front cover. You know the sort of thing.'

'Wish they'd leave me alone,' said the editor. 'All right, fair enough. Where's the copy?'

'Copy?'

'The spiel. The text. The *words*.'

'Oh! Er – it's – um – coming.'

'When?'

'Er – when do you need it?'

'Now.'

'What! I mean – oh. Yes, of course. I'll – um – get it. Now. I'll go and bring it. Okay?'

'Well, don't be long. This ain't the *Pigeon Fancier's Gazette*, you know. There's layout and layout, and we got *layout*, you know what I mean?'

'Gosh, I should say so,' said Henry, who hadn't the faintest idea. 'Layout. Mm. Right. Well, I'll get it along straight away.'

'You do that,' said the editor. 'Ta-ta.'

The school secretary was a sharp-edged character called Mrs Blanchard, and at first she didn't believe the desperate voice on the phone.

'No, Jacob – yes, that one – I've got to speak to him now – it's urgent – honestly –'

No-one rang up school to speak to kids; that was unheard of. Still, she shot off and hauled Jacob out of General Studies, to the teacher's relief, and then watched him closely as he answered the phone in her office.

'What?'

'Jake? Is that you?'

'Yeah.'

'It's Henry. Listen. They need some copy. Some spiel. You know, some *words*, to go with the pictures.'

'Oh, right. Okay.'

'Now! I mean sort of right away!'

'What?'

'Well, there's layout and layout, you see.'

'Oh.'

'So what shall I do?'

'Oh, yeah. Right. Well, leave it to me. What's your number?'

'I'm in a phone box!'

'Oh, blimey. Well, look, ring me at home, right, at half-past four. I gotta go. Okay?'

'But – but –'

Jacob rang off. Mrs Blanchard was pretty tough, and he didn't want any arguments with her, so he just said thank you and shot back to the classroom, where the teacher was trying to get them interested in some crummy old advertisements for soap.

Jacob slid back into place at the table and said 'Right, listen, this is urgent. We need some copy for Henry. Some *words*, right.'

'How much?' said Deirdre. 'How many words?'

'I dunno. There's layout and layout, see.'

'What's he talking about?' said David. 'We ought to

68

lay *you* out, Gaf.'

'Your trouble is you got no sense of responsibility,' Jacob said passionately. 'There's Henry stuck waiting for copy and you just make jokes. And they ain't funny, either. I'm disgusted.'

'What pictures are they going to use?' said Prakash.

'I dunno. All of 'em, maybe.'

'Right,' said Deirdre. 'Now shut up. Just belt up, right, and I'll do it. But I don't want to hear a *word*.'

So they all shut up. Since there was nothing to do while Deirdre scribbled, they had to listen to the teacher instead. The poor woman nearly wept with gratitude.

'Hello? Jake?'

'Henry?'

'Yes! Have you got it?'

'Yeah. You got something to write on?'

'Yes. But I've only got 50p to put in the box. You'll have to be quick.'

'Right. You ready?'

'Yes. Fire away.'

'Okay. Here we go. Right. "The Mighty Gobbo." That's the title.'

' "The Mighty Gobbo . . ." Okay. Got it.'

'And here's the copy. "It isn't often that a new star of *cool* hits the pages of *New Modes*. Nor the streets, for that matter. Anyone would think there was some secret underground organization trying to keep the cool waves under control." That's the first paragraph, right?'

' "– under control." Right. Got it, Jake. I say, this is hot stuff. What's next?'

'New paragraph, okay. "But no-one can control the mighty Gobbo. This new star is the coolest thing in the universe – and that's official." That's the end of another paragraph.'

' "– that's official." Okay. Fine. What's next?'

' "Last Saturday morning Gobbo was unveiled for the first time. With the brilliant new syndicate, How To Be Cool, and the world's first and only Coolometer, he gave the universe a taste of styles to come." End of the paragraph.'

' "– styles to come." Right. Carry on.'

'This is the last paragraph, right. "So if there *is* a secret underground organization, we bet it's full of creepy old men with weird eyes, and we bet they're running around in a panic right now, wondering where all the cool waves are coming from. But one thing's for sure – they ain't gonna stop. The mighty Gobbo and How To Be Cool are here to stay!" '

' "– here to stay." Exclamation mark?'

'What's one of them?'

'Never mind. I say, Jake, this is terrific. Did you write it?'

'No. Deirdre done it. You reckon it's okay?'

'I should say so! My word! We're really throwing down the gauntlet, aren't we?'

'Are we?'

'My goodness, this'll really hit 'em where it hurts. I'll get it up to the editor straight away.'

'Right. See you tomorrow, okay?'

'Same time, same place?'

'Yeah. And Henry?'

'Yes?'

'Ta.'

Louise couldn't work things out at all. Why hadn't Jacob been arrested? Why was he so pleased with himself? She kept giving him odd looks and making weird remarks until even their dad noticed and told her to belt up. She promised herself she'd get to the bottom of it if it killed her, and she kept hanging about and listening at his door, but she still couldn't work it out.

For the rest of that week they kept out of sight. Henry told them what Sandra had told him about the chaos in the Ops Room, and Prakash got dead worried. He got hold of his electronic-freak mates and they started to work on it. Nings called them the dandruff squad. They were very tall and bendy, with glasses and big Adam's apples, and no-one could understand a word they said. They took the Coolometer to pieces and spread it around David's garden, where they'd taken it to stop Louise interfering, and pretty soon they'd worked out what was happening. Apparently the copper tube sticking out of the bottle of water, which was acting as a radiator to stop the whole thing overheating, was amplifying and demodulating the heterodyne frequencies of the digital input from the coathangers, and simultaneously the 30,000 megahertz coaxial amplifier interface was boosting all the low-frequency cool waves in the 49 meter band. The solution was to put more water in the bottle, which damped it right out.

Jacob realised he had to keep everyone on their toes. So while Julie started working out some more cool for Gobbo, and Deirdre got stacks more copy written in case of interviews, and Gobbo kept sneaking off to play football and David and Nings kept fetching him away in case he dented his cool, and Prakash and the dandruff squad kept fiddling with superheterodyne bi-channel logic membranes and semiconductor-integrated cool-seeking capacitors, not to mention the dashboard light from his uncle's van, Jacob bombed around from one to another keeping them all busy, and Henry kept him in touch with all the panic inside the Cool Board.

And they all waited impatiently for Friday, when *New Modes* came out.

71

8

YOU KNOW WHAT THESE
CONTRACTS ARE LIKE . . .

'*New Modes* – you got any left?'

'There's one. You're in luck, son. Been a run on *New Modes* today.'

It was the third newsagent Jacob had tried. Louise had grabbed the papers before he'd had a chance to look at them, and he didn't want to show her how much he wanted to see *New Modes*, so he'd bombed out of the house as soon as he'd had breakfast.

And there it was! *The Mighty Gobbo* all over the cover! Jacob stood there in the middle of the pavement and read the whole thing. They'd used seven of the pictures, and all the copy was there. They'd done it!

Jacob leapt on his bike and shot off to school.

In the playground there was a struggling bunch of small girls around Gobbo, all wanting him to sign their copies of *New Modes*, and he was blushing like the top of a traffic light.

Jacob shoved his way through and said 'No interviews, right? Anyone asks you for an interview, you clear it with me and Deirdre first.'

'Interviews?' said Gobbo, and he changed colour again, to white this time. 'Who's going to interview me, Gaf?'

'TV, radio, papers,' said Jacob loudly, so that all the small girls could hear. 'You just tell 'em to contact the management.'

72

'What management?' said one of the lovestruck weenies. 'Are you his manager?'

'The management of How To Be Cool,' Jacob told her. 'You read the copy, have you?'

'What copy?'

'The spiel. The *words*. There's words in there and all, you know. You read that. Any interviews you want with the mighty Gobbo, you clear it with me. See you, Gob ...'

He raced inside to find the others all peering at a copy of the magazine spread out on Julie's desk. The teacher was trying to take the register, but she might as well have been giving them a lecture on porridge for all the attention she was getting. Finally Gobbo came in, looking bashful, and there was a huge cheer, so the teacher gave up altogether and guessed. Then the bell went, and they all slumped out to Design.

The atmosphere inside the Cool Board was tense. Everyone except Mr Cashman had seen *New Modes*, but no-one had dared mention it to him until Sylvianne had taken the magazines in with his coffee.

Being Sylvianne, she didn't realise anything was wrong, and started prattling about the brilliant pictures in *New Modes*.

'I *love* the yellow socks, Mr Cashman,' she said.

'Yellow socks?'

Mr Cashman looked down at his ankles, but they were grey and woolly. Was she colour-blind or something?

'And as for the teddy-bear –'

'What are you talking about, girl?'

'*New Modes*, Mr Cashman. The Mighty Gobbo! I think he's wonderful ...'

Mr Cashman snatched the magazine off the tray, sending his coffee flying. Alarm bells were ringing in his head: teddy bears weren't scheduled for two years yet. His eyes bulged when he saw the cover, and when he read the copy, they practically came out like yo-yos.

'Who – what – how –' he spluttered.

Sylvianne pressed one hand to her bosom, held the other palm outwards at shoulder height, and opened her sensational mouth wide. That was all supposed to express shock and horror. It was a pity Mr Cashman didn't see it.

Instead, he tore *New Modes* in half and banged his fist down on the desk. The veneer sprang off with a twang, and all three telephones and the executive toy flew six feet in the air. The ball-bearings cascaded everywhere – on Mr Cashman's head, down Sylvianne's dress, in the coffee-pot, all over the place.

They hadn't taught her to cope with that sort of thing in the Training Centre, so she slid to the floor and tried to faint. Mr Cashman took no notice; he plunged into the chaos and made straight for the door, bellowing strange oaths.

Unfortunately, he put his foot right on half a dozen ball-bearings. He was going quite fast at the time, and when he next got in touch with the floor, he did it with his head. He suddenly lost interest in *New Modes* and teddy bears and everything else.

A deep peace descended on the office. Sylvianne looked at the devastation with horror.

Design was a drag. There was no metal left to do metalwork with, and the kiln was broken so they couldn't do pottery either. The only thing there was plenty of was needles, so the class all had to sit around sewing, and there was no chance to doss about, because the guy in charge was a real hornet. He could have given Mr Cashman a good run in any meanness contest.

Gobbo was just putting the last stitch into the filthy

piece of rag he'd been working on. His design said
M A N U N T I E D.

'There,' he said, satisfied. 'Look at that, lads.'

They did.

'Who's going to tell him?' said David after a moment.

'But no-one had a chance to, because just then
Mrs Blanchard the secretary came in and spoke to the
teacher, who looked round and beckoned to Gobbo
with a mean little finger.

'The Headmaster would like a word with you,' he
said. 'Go on, hurry up.'

'No interviews, Gob,' Jacob said. 'You tell him
straight.'

Gobbo must have done, because within five minutes
he was back for Jacob and Deirdre.

'What's he want? What's he want?' Jacob demanded
as soon as they were out of the Design room.

'I dunno. He had the magazine on his desk and he
wanted to know what it was all about, like. I said you
was in charge.'

'Hmmm,' said Jacob. 'What d'you reckon?' he asked
Deirdre.

'He's no problem,' she said, meaning the Head. 'He's
just a nuisance.'

The Head was a helpless kind of guy who spent all his
time organising fêtes and jumble sales and barn dances
and showing parents round the school. He never did
any teaching that Jacob was aware of; perhaps he didn't
actually know anything. If you got into real trouble it
was terrible, because the Head had you in his office and
cried. He actually wept real tears to show you how
much you'd upset him. You had to be a real hard nut to
stand up to that kind of thing. Jacob had a strange
feeling about this summons: he couldn't work out
whether they were going to be wept at or crawled to,
and he didn't like it.

The Head met them at the door of his office, a big dopey beam on his face.

'The Mighty Gobbo!' he said.

Gobbo shuffled his feet.

'And Debbie! And Jason!' the Head went on.

They looked at each other: was it worth correcting him? Probably not, on the whole.

'Come in, come in,' he was saying. 'Tell me all about it! This is a wonderful achievement ...'

There was some anxious-looking teacher waiting to see him as well, but he bustled her out of the way and got her to fetch a couple of chairs for Jacob and Deirdre.

'Thank you, Miss Cartwright, thank you so much – no, later, I'll see you later, this is very important – oh, you had an appointment for now? Well, you'll just have to see Mrs Blanchard and make another one – yes, yes. Well, kids,' he said finally, as the poor woman crept out. 'Great!'

And he sat down on the floor.

Jacob and Deirdre could hardly believe their eyes, and when they looked at each other you could practically see the *think* bubbles above their heads saying WEIRD. Then they noticed that he had white socks on as well. The poor deluded man thought he was being cool.

'Well then,' he said, 'Tell me all about it. We're going to hit the big-time, eh? Triff!'

Gobbo shuffled his feet again and looked at Jacob. Jacob just shrugged; he'd never been so embarrassed since they made him play the Fairy Prince in his infants' school play. But Deirdre wasn't going to talk. It was up to him.

'It's a joke,' he said feebly.

'Oh! Ha ha! Brill!' chortled the Head. 'Well, you've certainly put the school on the map, Jason. We'll have a spread of all the pictures on the Achievement Board – how about that? Let the whole world know!'

Jacob felt Deirdre get tense beside him. The Achievement Board was where they stuck things like Ballet Club certificates and Chess Club results. The Head kept sticking up notices about himself, too, saying things like 'Mr Staines has (finally) passed the minibus test!' or 'Mr Staines came to school by bike instead of by car on 52 days out of 70 last term!' There was a photo from the paper showing him in the School Health Week Fun Run, looking like a gigantic bean bag with shorts and a beard.

No, there was no doubt about it. If they went up on the Achievement Board, they were finished.

'We – er – we can't – er – I mean it's – sort of copyright,' Jacob said desperately.

'Nonsense!' said Mr Staines heartily. 'Newspapers don't mind being quoted. In fact they love it. Tell you what – we'll write and ask them for the original photos. How about that, Raymond? Real glossy photos!'

Gobbo was so unused to being called by his real name that he didn't take any notice. He was busy trying to poke a hole in the carpet with his toe. Then Deirdre spoke up – about time too, Jacob thought.

'No, Mr Staines,' she said, 'Jacob's right. We had to sign a contract. The magazine has to ... sort of ...'

'Give permission,' Jacob said quickly. 'Else we'd be breaking the law. I mean we'd like to help you, but –'

'What about Raymond? Gombo, I mean?' said the Head. 'Have you signed a contract, Gombo?'

'Course he has,' said Jacob, desperate to stop Gobbo telling the truth. 'Only he ain't called Gobbo on it. That's just a professional name.'

'You know what these contracts are like,' Deirdre said.

Mr Staines had once been interviewed by the local radio station when the school was closed for the boiler to be repaired. He reckoned he knew quite a lot about the media.

'Oh, contracts,' he said, 'I could tell you a thing or two about contracts. Still, I tell you what. We'll write to the magazine anyway – invite them to come down here and do a feature. How about that? It's a pretty cool school, all things considered. There's the Morris Dancing Club, and the Duke of Edinburgh's Award Winners Appreciation Society –'

Jacob felt as if a pit of nameless horror had opened up just about where his breakfast was. But then Deirdre came to the rescue.

'That's a good idea, Mr Staines,' she said. 'But you better say the National Cool Board authorised it. Don't use our names at all.'

Jacob felt the nameless horror vanish at once. That was brilliant! Let the Cool Board take all the shame!

'National Cool Board?' said Mr Staines.

'That's what the organization's called,' said Jacob. 'Tell 'em the Cool Board says it's okay, only don't mention us. We don't want to grab all the headlines,' he added modestly.

'Yeah,' said Gobbo. 'Right.'

'Well then,' Jacob said, getting up, 'We better go then, Mr Staines. We got lots of sewing to do.'

'Brill!' said the Head enthusiastically. He floundered up off the floor and showed them out just as the bell rang for break. He brushed aside a group of teachers standing about with their diaries waiting to see him, and made straight for the phone in the school office.

'Get me London,' he said to Mrs Blanchard. 'Right away.'

Jacob and Deirdre exchanged another look. Had they done the right thing? Had they made a mistake?

Then they looked at the Achievement Board, and shook their heads. No, they hadn't made a mistake; anything was better than that.

Of all the pictures of Gobbo in *New Modes*, none of them attracted more attention from the keen followers of style than the ones featuring his feet. One particular close-up showed him wearing tan suede desert boots and yellow socks. The shattering beauty of this combination struck a hundred thousand pairs of eyes at once, and by lunch-time on Saturday every pair of yellow socks in the country had been snapped up by style-hungry dudes, and the shops were clamouring for more.

The Manufacturing Division of the Cool Board just couldn't cope. They were still turning out white socks by the million, and in an effort to save the situation, they tried to switch the sock machines over to yellow; but in their panic they got the programs wrong, and the machines extruded long yellow tubes with no feet, some of them hundreds of yards long.

Sylvianne walked around all week on tiptoe speaking very quietly; the Security Guards pulled their crash helmets even further down over their eyes; and three Cool Agents and two Detrendifiers got the sack for turning up to work in yellow socks.

In fact, things were getting desperate.

On Thursday afternoon, Henry turned up at the Rec with a letter.

It had come to the office of *New Modes*, he said, and the editor had passed it on to him. It was addressed to *How To Be Cool*, and the envelope showed it had come from Metropolitan TV.

'What's it say? What's it say?' said Nings, as Jacob scrabbled at the envelope and pulled out a big sheet of paper.

'"Dear How To Be Cool,"' Jacob read, '"I *love* the Mighty Gobbo. I love the whole concept. I *love* it.

Ring me and we'll talk about a spot on *Street Noise*. Yours, Ronnie Larkin, Producer, *Street Noise*."'

'It's a trap,' said David at once. 'Don't touch it.'

'You gone nuts?' said Nings. 'They're offering us a spot on the telly! They're *offering* us! We can't turn that down.'

'Wow,' said Gobbo. 'What we going to do, Gaf?'

'Leave it to me,' said Jacob. 'Deirdre and me'll work it out. We got to do this right, else we'll be in dead trouble. If this goes wrong it could be worse than the Achievement Board, even. We're not going to do *nothing* till we got it all worked out. Now get lost so's I can think about it.'

But an evening's thinking didn't make it any clearer, and when he got to school next morning he had a steaming headache from trying to work out whether it was a trap or not. The only thing that gave him any satisfaction was looking at the numbers of yellow socks around. One or two of the dudes in the upper forms had even managed to find some suede boots from somewhere. Things were looking up.

Then came a bombshell. Halfway through a Maths lesson he got yanked out to see the Head. He thought: What've I done now? Is he going to cry at me? Or has *New Modes* told him to get lost?

The Head was rubbing his hands at the door. 'Come in, Jason,' he said joyfully. 'We've got a visitor for you!'

He closed the door behind them as a creepy voice said 'Hello, Jacob. How nice to see you again. I hope you're well ...'

Jacob felt as if all his ribs had unzipped and fallen in a clattering heap down in his stomach somewhere. Because sitting in the Head's chair, blinking like a lizard, was Mr Cashman.

9

NOT FOR A MILLION QUID

Gulp . . .

'Oh, hello, Mr Cashman,' said Jacob. 'Haven't seen you for a couple of weeks.'

'Have you been keeping well, Jacob?'

'Yes, thanks. You had an accident, have you, Mr Cashman?'

Mr Cashman's left foot was in plaster, and there was a large Elastoplast on the top of his head. Mr Cashman frowned and looked shifty. Aha, Jacob thought.

'Nothing major,' said Mr Cashman. 'Kind of you to ask.'

The Head was standing dithering at one side, and Jacob decided to show Mr Cashman who was the boss around here, so he turned and said, 'Mr Cashman and me's got some business to discuss, Mr Staines. We'll be all right in here, thanks.'

'Right! Triff!' said Mr Staines. 'Right on, Jason! I won't disturb you.'

He tiptoed past Mr Cashman, grabbed a pile of papers from his desk, and tiptoed out and shut the door.

Jacob sat in the Head's own chair, and swung masterfully round to face Mr Cashman. Mr Cashman gave a cold, creepy smile, and the masterful feeling shrivelled up at once.

'Right,' said Mr Cashman. 'Now I happen to know that you've had an invitation to appear on *Street Noise*.'

'So what?'

'So don't, that's what. This is a friendly warning: stay away from that show, or else. However, to show our fundamental goodwill, I'm prepared to make you an offer. That agent of yours – what's he called – the Mighty Gobbo. You sell him to us, we take him off your hands and run him properly, it'll be easier all round, and you'll be nicely in pocket.'

'What d'you mean – buy him?'

'Straightforward transfer deal. Happens all the time. Standard contract.'

'How much?'

'Interested, then?' said Mr Cashman. 'Thought you might be. Of course, if that deal goes through, there's always the chance of more. We might be in the market for some new technology – electronics – telecommunications – that kind of thing. I'm sure you know what I mean.'

Here, thought Jacob, he's on about the Coolometer – they've discovered cool waves – he'll want to buy Prakash next – brain drain – blimey – I could make a fortune . . .

The air seemed to be full of little flickering £ signs. He blinked. Get a grip on yourself, he thought. What would Deirdre say?

'So you're worried then,' he said.

'Worried? Ho ho, if you think we're –'

'It's obvious. You're dead nervous. Well, I tell you what, Mr Cashman. You go back to the Cool Board and I'll discuss it with my associates and let you know our answer by this time next week. Course, we'll have to know what sort of money we're talking about. What's your offer?'

Mr Cashman snarled and leant forward. Jacob felt his skeleton try to get up and make a run for it, but he kept it under control.

'Listen, son,' Mr Cashman said. 'I'll tell you what my

82

offer is. Co-operate, and there'll be peace all round, and you can go back to playing football and wearing pink shirts. But you go near that TV show and you'll regret it.'

'Why?'

'You'll find out. We've got resources, young man.'

'You talking about the Detrendifying Squad?' Jacob said. He didn't like the way this conversation was going at all.

'What do you know about the Detrendifying Squad?'

'I'll tell you one thing,' said Jacob, making it up desperately, 'I bet you anything you like that some of 'em are wearing yellow socks and desert boots. You better start checking, Mr Cashman. And all them Security Guards – you checked their socks lately? And you sure you ain't got any teddy bears in the Cool Board? And what about –'

'All right,' said Mr Cashman, getting to his foot. 'If that's the way you want to play it. My offer's open till Wednesday. You know where to find me – and now,' he added meaningfully, 'I know where to find you. That wasn't very smart, was it, using the name of the National Cool Board. You might have known we'd trace it.'

He limped across the floor. Jacob sat and sweated.

'Thank you, Mr Staines,' Mr Cashman called. 'We've concluded out little bit of business.'

The Head came whiffling in, rubbing his hands together.

'Jolly good! Right on!' he said. 'Care to stay to lunch, Mr Cashman? Like to see round the school? Cup of coffee? School magazine?'

'I must be on my way,' said Mr Cashman, smiling like a shark. 'Goodbye, Jacob.'

Jacob shook the hand he held out.

'You mind you don't run into any more accidents,

Mr Cashman,' he said. 'I expect it's all the strain and tension you're under at the moment. You want to spend more time playing with your executive toy. All them ball bearings are bound to relieve your feelings.'

With a final snarl, Mr Cashman snatched his hand away and stomped off growling.

The Maths teacher was standing in front of the class mumbling some weird gibberish and making strange marks on the blackboard, and his trousers were clinging on under his belly by a miracle. One of these days they were bound to fall. About the only point of interest in Maths lessons was seeing how far they slid down before he hitched them up again. David had started a nice little line of business taking bets on whether or not they'd hit the deck.

So when Jacob got back to the classroom he could tell by the concentration that the trousers were on the slide again. He had a quick look, and blinked. Surely they'd never got that far before? They ought to keep a record. Maybe a felt-tip pen – sneak up and draw a line on him – write the date – no, better not.

He sat down and whispered to Deirdre:

'That was Mr Cashman.'

'*What?*'

'He wants to buy Gobbo.'

'How much for?'

He shot her a look of approval. That had been his first reaction, too.

'He wouldn't say. He was well scared,' he said.

Under cover of the endless drone about equations and y-values and the continuing gravity-driven trouser-creep, Jacob told her everything that had happened.

'Wow,' she said. 'He really is worried.'

'You bet. And I'll tell you something else –'

But just then the state of the trousers connected with

the state of the brain, and the teacher reached down and hitched them up. A collective sigh ran round the classroom; everyone felt free to move again; 45p changed hands and ended up in David's pocket.

'Where've you been, man?' said Nings, waking up from the trance and finding Jacob back.

So Jacob had to go through it all again for him and David and Prakash, and at the end of it Prakash said:

'We gonna do the telly, then?'

'Course. We got to, ain't we?'

'We going to put the Coolometer on?'

'No,' Jacob said. 'We'll keep that secret for the time being.'

'Just as well,' said Prakash. 'I been discovering stacks more about the waves. They're even more fundamental than I reckoned at first. They could be the biggest scientific discovery of *all time*, man.'

'Oh,' said Jacob. 'Smart.'

'How much was he offering for Gobbo?' said David.

'He never said. What d'you reckon he's worth?'

Putting a price on Gobbo kept them busy for the rest of the lesson. The Maths teacher was aware that he'd lost the class's attention somehow, but he couldn't work out where he'd gone wrong. Maybe the x-values of the equation should have been … Or the differential matrix of the y-mode …

He turned back to the blackboard and burbled away happily till the bell went.

Something was up, Gobbo thought.

Or, since he was Gobbo, he didn't actually think it; he just sensed the five pairs of eyes on him in the playground and felt uncomfortable.

He wasn't even sure that they *were* eyes. They looked more like £ signs.

'Here,' he said feebly. 'What's going on?'

85

With an effort the £ signs cleared themselves.

'Oh, nothing, Gob,' said Jacob.

'Okay, Gobbo?' said Nings.

'Yeah. Why?'

'You're looking pretty cool today, Gobbo,' said David.

'Oh,' said Gobbo. 'Right.'

He didn't like the way Nings was walking round and round sort of measuring him with his eyes, and when Julie turned up and had to have it all explained to her, he couldn't believe his ears. A transfer fee! He might be worth millions!

For some reason Julie didn't like the idea.

'You're not going to let him go and work for *them*?' she said. 'You *nuts* or something? What you *thinking* of? They only want Gobbo 'cause they know he's cooler than anyone they've got. What are *we* going to do if we sell him? Give up or something? And they'd only put him in *New Modes* doing flower-arranging. I bet that's what they'd do. We can't sell Gobbo. It's ridiculous.'

They looked a bit ashamed then, apart from Julie, who was looking all hot. Gobbo felt a nameless fear squirming about inside him like a ferret in a pair of trousers. Flower-arranging! That was enough for him.

'I ain't gonna be sold,' he said firmly. 'I ain't doing flower-arranging for no-one, right. Not for a million quid, no way, man, *never*, okay? You understand? You get it?'

'Oh, Gobbo!' said David, fluttering his hands. 'You look so *cool* when you're angry! You're irresistible!'

'Yeah, well then,' Gobbo mumbled. 'Right.'

'Stop wasting time,' Jacob said. 'We ain't selling anyone. We're gonna *beat* 'em. So we got to do this telly thing and we got to work it all out before we ring the guy up, so they do what we want and we don't end up filling in five minutes at the end of the programme like some crummy amateurs. Okay. This needs planning. Julie, you got to work out what everyone's gonna wear. It's not just Gobbo this time, it'll be all of us. We got to work out *everything* . . .'

That evening, they all watched *Street Noise* to see the sort of thing they'd be up against. They watched it most weeks anyway, but it felt different this time.

There were two presenters, a blonde girl called Delilah who tried hard to be wacky and zany and wild, and a black guy called Winston who tried even harder to be sleepy and sexy and cool.

'Pair of fakes,' said Deirdre. 'We'll sort them out.'

In fact the whole show was a fake. Delilah and Winston pretended that everything was happening at the last minute and they didn't know what was going to be on the show, but since the same kind of things happened every week you'd have thought they'd know what to expect by this time. There were always a couple of new pop videos, one near the start and the other near the end. There was always a guest for Delilah to talk to, and she always pretended to be just *amazed* that it was actually *him* and he was really *there* and could she touch him else she'd never *believe* it? And there was always a female guest for Winston to chat up, and he'd be all sophisticated and intimate and they'd sit on a big sofa and the camera would come right up close and the *soul* would be just pulsating in his big sleepy eyes. He looked like Jacob's dog Mouldy after Jacob had given him a pickled onion to eat once, just before he was sick on the carpet.

Then there was a spot where Delilah got taken out by some blushing bunch of blokes and shown how to water-ski or ride a camel or something. And whatever happened she'd always shriek and fall off. You were supposed to think what a great character she was, and how funny she was being, and what a great time you were having watching her.

'Right,' said Jacob after Delilah had fallen out of her canoe and Winston had chatted up this week's quivering victim, 'I can see what we got to do. Deirdre, you get on the phone and ring up this Larkin geezer. And what you tell him is this . . .'

10

I'VE GOT YOU NOW, CREEP

It was a heavy week. About twenty different things were all happening at once, and each of them was focused on *Street Noise*.

Mr Cashman was desperate to stop Jacob and the rest appearing on it. He racked his brains, and then he remembered that one of the spots in the show featured a fake street with a lot of kids hanging about being streetwise and showing off the latest styles. He decided to get them replaced by hard nuts from the Detrendifying Squad. A bunch of them got rounded up and herded into the Ops Room for a special briefing.

'Now, boys,' said Alex, with Mr Cashman standing behind him, 'get this clear. The minute any of these How To Be Cool kids comes on, give 'em the works. The jeer, the raspberry, the boo. You'll know who they are, cause they'll announce themselves. This one's called the Mighty Gobbo ...'

He pressed a button, and a picture of Gobbo from *New Modes* appeared on a screen.

'He's their number one agent,' Alex told them. 'He's dangerous, so watch him. And this one ...'

He pressed the button again and a picture of Jacob came up. He hadn't been in *New Modes*, so Mr Cashman had had to take it in the Head's office with a miniature camera concealed in his plaster cast.

'I know it ain't very clear,' said Alex, 'but take a good look at it all the same. The geezer's called Jacob. He's their boss. He's cunning, he's unscupr – unscrulop – unslu ... dangerous, and he's as slippery as an eel. As for the rest, we ain't got pictures of them. But this Jacob's the number one target. If he gets anywhere near the screen – move in and get him. If they start interviewing the Mighty Gobbo – stage a diversion. Right?'

The Detrendifiers nodded. They were all small and hard and bony, with faces like elbows; they reckoned they could sort out a few amateurs with no trouble. But then Mr Cashman took over.

'Men,' he said, 'I don't want to conceal anything from you. The National Cool Board is facing the greatest crisis in its history. Our great organization is on the brink of either enormous success or humiliating failure. Are we to be frustrated by a desperate band of terrorist style setters? Let us go onward, men! Let us regain the leadership, the trend-setting mastery of style that once was ours! Do not fail, men. Our future is in your hands.'

He waited for applause. But as well as having faces like elbows, the Detrendifiers had brains like knees. Alex had to step in and say 'Get 'em, lads!' before they realised what he was on about.

'Yer,' they said. 'Yer, yer ... Get 'em, yer.'

Unnoticed in the corner, Sandra scribbled it all in her poetry book. Her eyes were wide with horror.

Deirdre fixed up a meeting between Jacob and the *Street Noise* producer for Monday afternoon at the Rec. He came up in his lime-green 1957 Cadillac, hoping to impress them.

Ronnie Larkin was a worried man. The viewing figures for *Street Noise* had been going down, and their audience research had shown that they were starting to pick up the wrong kind of viewers anyway. The show was getting more and more popular with grannies and under-eights and less and less popular with the real stylists. Sometimes Ronnie Larkin reckoned it was Delilah's stunts causing the problem, and then he thought maybe Winston was running out of soul; or it might have been the kids on the 'street' – they all seemed kind of second-rate these days – he couldn't work it out.

It was worth a trip up to look at How To Be Cool, anyway.

Then Jacob told him what they wanted. He was stunned.

'But – but that would change the whole *concept* of the show,' he said.

'About time,' said Deirdre.

'D'you think so?'

'Yeah,' said Prakash. '*Street Noise* is going right down, man. Even my Grandma watches it now.'

Since that was just what the audience research had told him, Ronnie Larkin had to listen to them. In the end he agreed to do what they wanted.

'I'm taking a *huge* risk,' he said. 'You don't *know* what a risk it is.'

'That's nothing compared to what we're risking,' Jacob said. 'You ain't heard of the National Cool Board, have you?'

'National Cool Board?'

'See,' Jacob said to the others. 'No-one's heard of it. That's how they kept going all this time. Well, we'll force 'em out in the open. You leave it to us, Mr Larkin. We'll be there on Friday. Just give us a list of the guests, and –'

'Thursday,' said Ronnie Larkin. 'We record the show on Thursday.'

'Well, we'll do it live,' Jacob told him. 'That'll be more exciting for you, won't it? You'll have all the thrill

91

of wondering whether we're going to turn up or not. Here's a list of what we want done. And remember – d'you want to be cool? Or d'you want to produce the weenies and grannies show?'

Ronnie Larkin gulped. He didn't have any choice, really.

'Now then, Alex,' said Mr Cashman across the newly-repaired desk. 'You said something about a sister.'

'Yeah,' said Alex. 'She's called Louise.'

'Nice girl? Attractive? Friendly?'

'Well,' Alex said, 'put like that, Mr Cashman, since you ask, to be frank – no.'

'Tough luck.'

'Eh?'

'I want you to make the closer acquaintance of this Louise. Chat her up. Take her out. Fascinate her, Alex. Worm your way into her girlish affections.'

'Ah. I get it.'

'She's bound to know what the boy's up to. Fill her up with cheese-burgers and Cheepicola and see what you can find out. They've got something special planned, and the TV company's keeping the lid on. Find out where and when and so forth, and we can get 'em. Don't let me down, Alex.'

'Okay, Mr Cashman,' said Alex glumly. 'Right.'

I didn't join the Cool Board for this, he thought, as he stomped out past the Security Guard at the door. Being made a monkey of by some kid – having to take out his guzzling Gorgon of a sister – it was enough to make you give up in despair.

Still, Alex had a stern sense of duty, and he didn't hesitate. Pausing only to scowl at three women who happened to be carrying identical shopping bags, he got on a bus and went off to hang around outside school and wait for Louise.

Meanwhile, Ronnie Larkin went through the list of guests for this week's *Street Noise*. Up till recently he'd had agents and managers of all kinds ringing him up and pestering him and buying him drinks just in order to get their stars on the show, but he was having to do the chasing these days, and he didn't like it.

'Well, Laura,' he said heavily when he got back from meeting Jacob, 'who've we got lined up? Anyone the punters will actually have heard of?'

'Lou Craggs,' said his secretary hopefully.

'Remind me! Remind me!'

'He's the star of that new adventure film – the one about the pilot who discovers the Aztec temple –'

'Oh, another one of those ... Who else?'

'Serenata.'

'Who?'

'The model.'

'Oh. For the Winston spot. Let's have a look ...'

His secretary passed over a bunch of photographs of a girl doing various modelling things. She was pretty amazingly beautiful, he thought.

'What's the angle on this one?' he said.

'She's dead clever. She's got all kinds of degrees and stuff.'

'Well, that should give Winston something to think about ...'

Then he remembered what Jacob had lined up for Winston, and shivered. Winston would have enough to think about without educated models.

'More,' he said. 'Who else?'

'Some old bloke called Jumpin' Joe King,' she said nervously.

'Jumpin' Joe ... What is this? *Recordbreakers* or something? *Street Noise* is the cutting edge of style, Laura! The state of the art! Who is this moribund athlete, for Heaven's sake?'

'He's not an athlete, Ronnie,' she said. 'He's – well, he was – well, he used to be quite famous.'

'What for? When?'

'Back in the 1940s. He was some sort of piano player or something. Sort of jazz, I think.'

'Wonderful. Sensational. If you're going to go out, go out with a bang. Book the studio for Friday, Laura, not Thursday. We're live this week. This is a special. We're calling it *How To Be Cool*. And now I'm going to lie down and take a pill. Don't bother to wake me up.'

Sometime soon, Jacob thought, he'd have to tell his parents that he wasn't going to be home on Friday evening. They'd all have to skip school that afternoon as well, but they could sort that out when the time came.

His usual method was to tell things like that to his dad. His mum never missed a trick, but his dad was either half asleep or too busy to listen properly. There was the Louise problem, too. He didn't want her overhearing. She was even more weird than usual these days – almost as if she was spying on him.

So he waited till his dad was in the garden and Louise was washing her hair, and then he pounced. His dad was prodding away at some miserable-looking plant when Jacob arrived. He looked up suspiciously.

'What do you want?' he said. 'Give me that hoe, will you.'

Jacob passed him a rake. 'Nothing,' he said. 'I don't want anything. Honest.'

His dad sighed. 'That is a rake. I want a hoe. And I don't believe you. What do you want?'

This wasn't going to be easy, Jacob thought. 'Is this the hoe?' he said, trying to sound interested.

'No,' said his dad. 'That is a fork. It has got prongs. See the nice prongs, Jacob! Hand it to me, and I shall do something with it which you will not like. What I want is the hoe. Give it to me, please, and then go and drive someone else mad.'

'Oh, this one,' said Jacob. 'Right. The hoe. I got it. What's it for?'

'Gardening with. Goodbye.'

'Yeah, but what do you do with it?'

'You get rid of unwanted intruders in the garden. You shove it under their roots and grub them up. Alternatively you swing it round your head and –'

'Yeah, all right,' said Jacob, moving out of range. 'Actually –'

'And get off the carrots!'

Jacob looked down. He was ankle-deep in a lot of green things.

'It's all right, Dad,' he said helpfully, 'these ain't carrots. Carrots are sort of red and pointy. This is grass or something. Anyway –'

'*Out!*' his dad roared. Jacob leapt out like a rocket. 'Now stand *there*,' his dad went on, thumping the ground with the hoe, 'and hurry up and tell me what you want so I can say no and start repairing the garden.'

'Oh, right,' Jacob said, and stood carefully where his dad told him. 'What it is, right, I got to go on the telly on Friday.'

'What?'

'There's this programme, okay, called *Street Noise*. And 'cause Gobbo was in this magazine and got famous they want us on the programme this Friday.'

'You mean you're going to be appearing on it?'

'Yeah.'

His dad laughed. 'That's the foul row Louise watches. Does she know you're going to be on it?'

'No. I don't want to tell her, either.'

'Sounds a good plan. What are you going to do on it?'

'Just talk about styles and that.'

'What, you? Talk? What you do to the English

95

language, I wouldn't do to a greenfly. Still, it'll give Louise a shock. That'll be worth watching. How are you going to get there? When are you getting back?'

So that was all right.

When he got inside, the phone rang.

'Yeah?' he said, answering it.

The line was crackling. He could hardly hear the voice at the other end.

'Gaf? Ronnie Larkin here. I just wanted to run through a couple of things – the guests on the show – can you hear me? There's a super line-up. We've got Lou Craggs, no less –'

'Blue bags? This is a terrible line, man –'

'*Lou Craggs*. The film star. And Serenata – you know, the model – she was on the cover of *Vogue* last month. And best of all, Gaf, how about this – Jumpin' Joe King!'

'Who's he then? A kangaroo?'

'He's only the best blues pianist of the 1940s, Gaf – a legend – a classic – he played with Louise Jordan, Cab Calloway, Slim Gaillard – everyone! He was the *tops* –'

'Oh, right. Where do we go?'

'Yes – good point. Glad you asked. Now normally we record in Studio Ten –'

'Studio Ten? I can't hear you, man – this is all crackling – did you say Studio Ten?'

'Yes – but we're not using it this week, because we're going out live – you come to reception and we'll meet you there. We'll be in Studio Fourteen. Listen, Gaf, I can't persuade you to do it on tape, I suppose?'

'What?'

'You won't record it on Thursday – is that final?'

'Dead final. We do it live on Friday or we don't do it at all.'

'Oh, very well . . . You realise how important this is?'

Blimey, Jacob thought, he sounds desperate. 'Course

I do,' he said. 'Stop panicking, man. This is How To Be Cool. We're in charge of style now, and it's no longer trendy to panic. That's official. See you Friday.'

He rang off and shot out to find Deirdre.

At the top of the stairs, Louise was crouching with a towel round her head. She'd been listening to everything Jacob had said. Most of it was gibberish, but there were some bits she did understand: there was a kangaroo involved, and some blue bags, and they were going to do it live on Friday in Studio Ten.

H'mm, she thought.

She was washing her hair in order to go out with Alex. After a couple of days hanging about, he'd spotted her coming out of school and moved in. He was wearing his white socks and low-cut black shoes, which was lucky for him, because ever since the yellow-sock-and-desert-boot style had hit the streets, Louise had regarded white socks and black shoes as the only sure sign of anti-Jacob-ness.

She was surprised to see them on Alex, though, because she still thought he was one of Jacob's drugs ring, and she was a bit suspicious at first. But after he'd given her a couple of cigarettes and they'd sneered at each other in the usual way, he asked her out and she said yeah, if you want.

He took her to see a Sylvester Stallone film. The effect of all those weird-looking muscles on Louise's brain was to make it even more confused than it normally was, and the flavour-enhancers and artificial colourings in the popcorn she kept shoving into her face completely zapped the little bit of sense she had left. By the time Stallone had killed the last communist and she'd absorbed the last chemical in the popcorn, she'd begun to see Alex in quite a different light. In fact, she very nearly fancied him.

97

And when she discovered on the way home (after two Pina Coladas, seven cigarettes, and three packets of gherkin-and-barbecued-spare-rib-flavour crisps) that Alex was actually as anti-Jacob as she was, if not more, she definitely fancied him.

She was too fuddled to understand what he was on about, but she decided to help. So she told him all about the phone call she'd overheard.

'Decent, Louise,' said Alex. 'That's well smart, that is. We can get him now. Here – why don't you come up with me and the boys and watch us sort him out?'

'Yeah,' she said. 'That'd be a laugh. I'll do that. Ta, Alex.'

And she thought as she smirked to herself later in bed: I've got you now, creep. You just wait till Friday.

11

COMPLETELY UNPROFESSIONAL

At a quarter to seven on Friday evening, the panic-count at the TV studios was astronomical.

For some reason, about a hundred and six things had all gone wrong at the same time. The reception staff were on strike, so visitors had to follow signs hastily scribbled on bits of paper and find their own way about the place; the producer of *Out For The Count*, a game show that was due to start recording at seven o'clock, was tearing his hair out because his promised audience couldn't get there as their coach had broken down, and his assistant hadn't managed to come up with anyone else yet; and as if that wasn't enough, a colossal row was going on in Studio Twelve.

It involved two actors who were both in love with the same actress. They were doing a sketch for some comedy show at the time, and one of them was dressed as a wallaby and the other was dressed as a tomato. The actress was sobbing wildly on the shoulder of the star, who was dressed as a pickled onion.

'We ought to be recording this,' said the sound man to the floor manager. 'It's better than the script.'

The actress heard, and wailed even louder.

In the *Street Noise* studio, on the other hand, everything was cool. In fact it was all a bit too cool for Ronnie Larkin, who was on his sixtieth cigarette already.

'Oh, come *on*, Gaf,' he pleaded, 'you must give me

some idea of what you're going to say – I mean it's completely *unprofessional* –'

'It's cool though,' said Jacob. He was being made up at the time. There was a beautiful girl doing sensational things to his face, and she kept asking him if it was okay, and letting him look in the mirror. Jacob never minded looking in mirrors; each time he looked, he seemed to have got cooler.

'But I've got to *know*,' Ronnie went on. 'I mean, after what you did to Delilah –'

'You said you wouldn't go on about that,' Jacob told him.

'Yes, but you must see –'

'How's that?' said the make-up girl softly. 'I've put just a *tinge* of the eye pencil on ...'

Jacob looked. '*Decent*,' he said. 'You're doing a good job. What's your name again?'

'Carol. Is that okay, then?'

'Carol. Right. Stick a bit more on, why not. Can't do any harm. What did you do to Gobbo?'

'Oh, Gobbo!' said Carol. 'He's *amazing*! I mean he's so sort of ... Keep still, that's it. You've got lovely eyes, Gaf.'

'Yeah, I know. Two of 'em. You made up anybody else famous, then?'

Ronnie had two cigarettes going now, one in each hand. He hadn't realised yet.

'Gaf!' he said. '*Please*! There's only ten minutes to go, and we haven't been through the Jumpin' Joe spot yet. Now when he comes on –'

'Oh yeah,' Jacob said. 'He's all right, Joe. I had a talk with him while you were sorting Winston out. He'll be okay – I told him what to do.'

'But the piano –'

'I thought he'd like a drink, so I showed him where the whisky was in that room up there. You shouldn't

100

have hidden it, Ron. He was pretty thirsty, you know.'

'What!' Ronnie leapt up. 'He's had the best part of one bottle already – what were you *thinking* of –'

He shot out, leaving both cigarettes. Jacob shook his head.

'It's not cool to panic,' he told Carol. 'He ought to get an executive toy to play with. Let's have another look . . .'

Meanwhile, the producer of *Out For The Count* was being called to the phone in Studio Ten. He was in a worse state than Ronnie, almost.

'Yes? Yes? *Yes?*'

'Archie here, Brian – I've got an audience!'

'Where? I want them *here*! *Now*!'

'They're on their way, don't fret. I had a devil of a job to find them. I ought to warn you –'

'I don't care if you mugged them and dragged them in off the street *personally*. Just get 'em here.'

'Okay, okay. But listen, Brian, they're not going to understand much of the show – they're foreign. And –'

'I don't care if they're Martians, they can be anything they like as long as they're *here* . . . All right. You better let me have the details for the warm-up man.'

'Well, it's an over-sixties club from somewhere called Dunkelhausen-am-Weser. They're doing the sights. They were going to see *Cats* but their agent hadn't booked it properly or something. And –'

'Holy Cow. That's all I need. They want *Cats*, they get *Out For The Count* . . .'

'Something else, Brian. There's a group of kids as well – they were booked in to see –'

'Anyone, Archie! But *now*!'

The producer slammed the phone down and bombed off to tell everyone that they had an audience at last.

Archie, at the other end of the line, scratched his head

and wondered if he should have mentioned the kids first. A hundred disappointed weenies whose horse show had been cancelled might be harder to manage than fifty German pensioners, now he came to think of it.

Oh, well. He put the phone down carefully and sloped off for a drink.

The coach the Cool Board had hired drew up in the car park. All the Detrendifiers flexed their muscles and turned their knobbly faces towards Alex, who was standing inside the door.

'Okay, lads,' he said. 'You know the drill. No mercy, no surrender. Up the Cool Board!'

'Yer,' came the answer. 'Cool Board – yer! Cool Board – yer!'

They all piled out. Louise was impressed. She was beginning to think that Alex was almost as cool as Andrew Ridgley.

'Right,' said Alex, when the Squad was milling about in the reception area. 'Where do we go now?'

'Studio Ten,' said Louise. 'That's what he said on the phone.'

'Where's that?'

'How'm I supposed to know?' she said, blowing a huge bubble of gum.

Alex banged the bell on the desk. The Detrendifiers were all picking leaves off the plastic plants and carving their initials in the Bolo-wood panelling.

'There ain't no-one here,' Louise said.

'I can see that, can't I? Hang on, there's a notice –'
His lips moved silently as he traced it with his finger.
'Got it! Studio Ten this way. Come on, lads!'

He grabbed Louise's hand and dragged her down the nearest corridor. The Detrendifying Squad swirled after them.

102

The wallaby-actor had had enough.

'I've had enough!' he yelled at the tomato-man.

'Enough to drink, I suppose you mean,' the actress put in.

'What!' the wallaby-man roared. '*You* can talk. The amount you put away would bankrupt a brewery.'

'Waaah!' she wailed, and flung her arms round the pickled onion.

'Terribly unprofessional,' the star murmured.

'Can't act, either,' said the tomato-man.

'*What*?' That was the wallaby-man. 'Who can't act?'

'You,' said the tomato-man. 'Look at the mess you made of the custard scene. Chaos! I mean how many rehearsals do you *need*?'

'Right,' snarled the wallaby-man. 'That does it.'

He leapt at the tomato-man and tried to find his neck so he could strangle him. But tomatoes not having any necks to speak of, he was out of luck.

Still, the impact knocked the tomato-man over backwards, and he rolled round and round a few times before he found his feet and scrambled up. The wallaby-man was having trouble with his own feet, though. They were so long that having got one twisted behind the other, he couldn't get it straight, and he thrashed about on the floor for some time before he could get up. Then he fell over his tail and hit the deck again, while the tomato-man was stuck in the doorway trying to get out. He'd have got caught if a friendly cameraman – about the only other person in the place who hadn't collapsed with laughter – hadn't shoved him through just as the wallaby-man got up for the second time.

Yelling some harsh remarks at the cameraman, the wallaby bounded through the door after the tomato, who was disappearing as quickly as he could waddle towards the lift.

It was five to seven. Gobbo, made-up, rehearsed, trembling, was on his way to the toilet for the fourteenth time when he saw something unusual.

First of all a long line of pensioners came trooping past. They were all draped in cameras, and they all carried plastic shoulder-bags with the name of some travel firm on them, and they were talking Russian or something.

Then a huge great tomato came belting round the corner. Some of the oldies couldn't get out of the way, and got knocked down. The tomato fell over as well, and rolled over and over, bellowing with panic and trying to find out where his feet were.

Amid the tumult, some of the pensioners were explaining it all to each other.

'Ho, ho! *Eine grosse Tomate*,' they were saying.

'*Ja, ja!*' they said. '*It's A Ker-nock Out, ja?*'

Some of them lifted their cameras to take pictures of it.

'*Es ist nicht It's A Ker-nock Out*,' someone said. '*Es ist Out For The Count, ja?*'

'*Das ist das gleiche*,' someone else said, as the tomato finally struggled to his feet.

'Out the way! Mind out!' he yelled, and shoved his way through the crowd. Not being able to look round, he still thought the wallaby-man was behind him, and waddled away at about 40 miles per hour.

'*Ho ho ho*,' the Germans were saying to one another. '*Der englisch Humor. Sehr komisch! Ho ho ho.*'

They all went limping off.

Wow, Gobbo thought.

It was three minutes to seven.

Alex and the Detrendifying Squad had got lost.

'It ain't my fault,' Louise kept saying. 'I *told* you it was down that way. If you don't bloomin' well listen,

104

that's your fault.'

She blew a petulant bubble and slumped against the wall.

They were at a kind of crossroads in the centre of the building. All the corridors looked the same, and since none of the Detrendifiers could be bothered to read, they hadn't taken any notice of the signs on the way.

'What we going to do, Alex?' one of them said.

'Shut up,' said Alex. 'I'm thinking.'

Louise idly picked some bubble-gum off her chin. Then she saw something that made her blink.

'Here,' she said. 'Look! There's a wotsit.'

She pointed down the corridor. All the knobbly little faces of the Detrendifiers turned to look.

At the end of the corridor stood a wallaby.

It was watching them hesitantly. If they hadn't been such a tough-looking bunch of nuts it would have come bounding up to them looking for the tomato, but ...

'Didn't your brother say something about a kangaroo?' said Alex.

'Yeah, on the phone,' Louise said. 'I forget what he said. But he mentioned a kangaroo all right.'

The wallaby-man was still hesitating. Alex leapt into action.

'Get him, lads!' he yelled.

'Yer! Get him! Right!' came the cry from the Detrendifiers, and they all set off towards him.

The wallaby-man's hesitation vanished. With a yell of terror he hopped round through a hundred and eighty degrees and bombed away as fast as he could, with a mob of Detrendifiers close on his tail.

It was two minutes to seven.

Laurie, the floor manager, came anxiously up to Ronnie Larkin. Ronnie had just prised Jumpin' Joe King away from his bottle and given him to Deirdre to look after.

'What is it now?' he said to Laurie. 'Where's *Gaf?* He was there a minute ago – where's he *gone?*'

He looked around distractedly. He could feel every second going past.

'I just wondered where you wanted the kids, Ronnie,' said Laurie.

'Kids? What kids? Oh, *no* –'

The studio door was flung open, and a hundred crazed weenies came in like a tidal wave. They were all about eight years old, and most of them were wearing jodhpurs and riding hats. Some of them, Ronnie noticed with the sharpness of nightmare, were carrying little whips.

A scream came bubbling up his throat, and he clutched at the nearest camera.

'Who – what – where –'

'They just came charging in, Ronnie! There's no-one on the desk – we couldn't stop 'em –'

A big hefty woman with red cheeks and a scarf over her head came striding up and seized Ronnie's hand.

'Frightfully decent!' she barked. 'Pym. Cynthia Pym. Brought 'em all the way up here – gymkhana cancelled! Damn bad show. Bloody decent of you chaps. Where do we sit?'

Ronnie felt his head swivelling loosely in its socket. Wherever he looked the place was crawling with horse-maddened kids. It was like a vision of ultimate horror – and it was thirty seconds to seven.

Then he saw Jacob.

'Gaf!' he screamed, and sweeping Miss Pym out of the way, he scrambled over half a dozen weenies to get to him. 'Gaf! Twenty-five *seconds!*'

'What's all these kids doing?' Jacob said disapprovingly. He'd been sorting a couple of things out with Jumpin' Joe King, and he could hardly hear himself think.

106

'Camera One! Get there *quick*! Get there *now*! There's twenty *seconds* left and we're *live* – you can't *do* this to me! Oh, oh, oh – 'Ronnie was wailing like a banshee, and dragging Jacob through clinging bunches of whips and jodhpurs towards the presenter's seat.

'Hey,' Jacob said, 'I'm not working with all these kids about the place. What'd you bring 'em here for?'

'They're nothing to do with me – they just burst in – oh, why did I ever ... What is it?'

Jacob had stopped in his tracks. The kids were nothing to do with Ronnie, and How To Be Cool certainly hadn't brought them along ... There was only one place they could have come from.

'The Cool Board,' he whispered, terrified.

'What? What? What?'

'Detrendifiers,' Jacob said, his legs like spaghetti. 'Miniaturised Detrendifiers ...'

Ronnie put his head in his hands and rocked back and forth, moaning. Laurie the floor manager struggled through the chaos and tried to shake Jacob out of his trance of horror.

'Gaf!' he yelled. 'You're on in five seconds!'

On the floor above, the German oldies were lining up by the door of Studio Ten, ready for *Out For The Count*. They were about to go in when they heard a strange noise in the corridor behind.

Having already been attacked by a giant tomato, you'd have thought they'd be prepared for most things, but they were still surprised when they saw a panic-stricken wallaby bounding towards them.

'*Hier kommt ein Känguruh*,' they said.

'*Nein! Er ist nicht ein Känguruh. Er ist ein Wallaby*,' they explained.

Up came the cameras again.

'*Der englisch Humor wieder. Ho ho ho*,' they were

saying, just when the wallaby-man got there.

He was looking over his shoulder at the time, and he hit them like a demolition crane. Five of them went down at once. The wallaby-man's tail lashed itself round another old guy's legs and whipped them away from under him, and the yells and the shrieks filled the corridor as the Detrendifying Squad came bombing around the corner and fell over them.

The only person still on her feet was Louise. She watched it all, transfixed, her jaw working round and round automatically as the struggles and the panic and the cries of the wounded rose higher and higher.

'Gotcha!' she heard Alex yell, and saw that he'd grabbed the wallaby-man's tail.

The wallaby-man screamed and lunged forward. There was a tearing sound, and the tail and half the back of his legs came away in Alex's hand as he bounded off to freedom. Alex cursed and lunged after him – but Louise grabbed his arm.

'Look!' she said.

'What? What?'

'Blue bags! They all got blue bags, ain't they?'

She pointed. All the Germans had blue plastic shoulder bags with some foreign words on them. Alex didn't know what she was talking about – and then he remembered what she'd overheard of Jacob's phone call.

'Oh yeah!' he said. 'Blue bags, right! Okay, lads,' he called, 'this is it. Forget the kangaroo – we're going in here.'

Louise shifted the bubble-gum to the front and stood there smugly as the Detrendifiers unscrambled themselves from the sobbing, trembling over-sixties club of Dunkelhausen-am-Weser and piled in and sat down to watch *Out For The Count*. Alex watched in satisfaction.

'Brilliant, Louise,' he said. 'Magic.'

He was so pleased that he turned and gave her a huge kiss. Unfortunately, that was the moment she chose to blow her biggest bubble yet. They were both well surprised.

It was seven o'clock.

12

STREET NOISE

Deirdre saw Jacob hesitating, and leapt across the studio towards him. The signature tune was nearly over – Ronnie Larkin was kneeling down beating his head on the floor – Jacob was backing away in terror as a miniature horse-freak came menacingly towards him –

Then she got there and gave him a colossal thump.

'What are you waiting for?' she said. 'Get *on*!'

She shoved him at the presenter's chair, and he fell into it just in time. The shock woke him up. Detrendifiers? What was he afraid of? He was cool, wasn't he?

He straightened the dark blue bow tie he was wearing with his tattersall-check shirt, and turned his eyes (glowing darkly with make-up) to the camera.

'Right,' he said. 'Hello, viewers. This is Gaf here. This is a special edition of *Street Noise* called *How To Be Cool*, and in a minute we're going to introduce you to the mighty Gobbo, so you can see what *cool* really is. There's no videos this week either. We looked at 'em earlier on and they were a load of rubbish. You may be wondering where Delilah and Winston are. Okay. Delilah's in hospital, right, because she broke her leg, but it was entirely her own fault. As for Winston, he's doing a trick. Come over here and have a look.'

He jumped out of the chair and belted across the studio floor, colliding with half a dozen surging horse-freaks.

'Nings!' he yelled. 'Come over here and give'em *the teeth!*'

Realising that he was on camera, he turned and gave it an Eric Morecambe-style grin.

'Bit of trouble here,' he said. 'Take no notice. Anyway, here's Winston, in this box, okay.'

He shoved a couple of weenies out of the way, and there was a great big box, all wrapped around with ropes and chains and padlocks. Through a little square hole in the side Winston's face was looking out, well puzzled. Full of soul, though.

'What he's doing, right,' Jacob explained, 'he's doing an escape trick like Houdini. He's got to get out of the box by the end of the show. Okay, Winston? I got a surprise for you. Up there – ' he pointed up – 'we got a six-ton weight.'

The camera looked up, so the viewers could see the weight dangling on the end of a rope. They could also see Winston looking alarmed and trying to peer up out of his box.

'Hey, man,' he said, 'you didn't say nothing about a six-ton weight, man.'

'Well, it ain't going to be there for long,' Jacob told him. 'There's a bottle of acid eating through the rope right now. You got about twenty-five minutes, I reckon. We'll come back in twenty-four and a half.' He moved away from Winston, and pointed up at the weight. 'Sizzle sizzle,' he said to the camera. 'Hee hee hee. Right, there's some boring stuff on this programme too, so let's get it over with first. And our first guest this evening is – '

He stopped and looked at a small child with a whip, who'd come into the picture with him.

'What do you want?' he said.

'Get stuffed,' said the weenie.

Jacob was about to take a swing at it, but then he

thought of something, and gave a cunning smile.

'Here,' he said, 'd'you want to play a nice game? There's a funny man over there in a box. You go and play with him, go on.'

The kid stared at him for a second or so, then nodded and vanished.

'Gotta stay cool,' Jacob told the camera. 'Right, let's get this interview over. It's some geezer, I forget his name, but he's being interviewed by the famous Deirdre!'

He flung his arm out sideways like the ring-master at a circus. When he reckoned that the viewers were seeing Deirdre, he bombed off to have another word with Jumpin' Joe King.

Meanwhile, Deirdre had appeared on the screen. She was wearing a white dress with a big red sash tied round it, and she was swinging back in a big squashy leather chair.

'Smart chairs, these,' she said to the camera. 'They go backwards and spin round and do all sorts. Anyway, I got to interview this bloke. Right. What's your name?'

Sitting opposite her was a handsome-looking bloke with a little black hairline moustache. He blinked, as if he wasn't expecting to be asked that.

'Lou Craggs,' he said. 'And you're Deirdre, right?'

'Right so far,' she said. 'Are you famous? Actually you don't have to answer that. Probably you are, right, else you wouldn't be here.'

'Oh, thanks,' he said. 'Are you famous?'

'Not as famous as the mighty Gobbo. What d'you do for a living?'

'Well, I guess I'm a movie star,' he said, laughing easily.

But Deirdre wasn't charmed.

'All right, what's the name of your latest film?' she said.

112

'What is this, some kind of test?' he said. 'No, I didn't mean that. My latest movie. Okay. Well, it's an adventure spectacular called – why, hi, kid!'

A female horse-freak had appeared from nowhere and was standing between him and the camera.

'What d'you want?' said Deirdre.

'I want to go to the toilet,' said the child.

'It's over there,' said Deirdre. 'Behind the box with the funny man in. No, he won't look. Go *on*.'

She shoved the weenie out of the picture.

'Hey,' said Lou Craggs, 'this is some show, Deirdre!'

'What's your film called?'

'Oh, yeah. Well, it's a Steven Spielberg production –'

'That don't mean anything,' Deirdre said severely. 'Every film these days is a Steven Spielberg production. I bet he never had nothing to do with it.'

'He certainly did!' Lou Craggs said hotly. 'He was not only executive producer, he also co-wrote the very fine script. It's gonna be a smash, believe me.'

'It won't be anything if you don't tell people what it's called,' Deirdre pointed out. 'What are you trying to hide, anyway?'

'Nothing! Whaddya mean, what'm I trying to hide? Look, I came here, I thought this was a serious kind of show, I try to – '

There was a high-pitched yell from somewhere in the background, and Lou Craggs jumped.

'What the hell's going on?' he said. 'What are all these kids doing?'

'They're miniature Detrendifiers,' said a voice, and Lou Craggs looked up to see Jacob standing beside him. 'It's all right. Nings is sorting 'em out. You finished interviewing him yet?' he said to Deirdre.

'He won't answer the questions,' she said.

'Well, don't waste any more time on him, then,' Jacob said. 'Do the film.'

'Hey!' protested Lou Craggs, but Deirdre took no notice.

'Right then,' she said to the camera. 'This is the bit where – '

A weenie came past picking its nose, and she smacked it. It ran away.

'When we were planning this show, right,' she went on, 'we reckoned you must be as fed up as us with all this power-gliding and speedboat-racing and stuff Delilah does, cause no-one can afford it unless they're stinking rich, and I dunno about you, but I don't get much of a thrill watching someone else messing about with a million pounds worth of machinery, right, so we thought we'd give her a change this week. We took her out to Braybrooke Road with Nings's truck.'

'And it's no good her moaning,' Jacob put in. 'We *told* her it didn't turn right. Anyway if she'd kept further in where it picks up speed past the launderette she'd have been able to turn into the car park. Even Gobbo can do that.'

'It's entirely her fault,' Deirdre said firmly. 'Anyway, here it is.'

As the director switched the film in, Ronnie Larkin took his hands away from his eyes and picked up one of the three cigarettes he'd got burning in the ashtray.

'I can't take it,' he was muttering. 'I'm through! I'm finished!'

'You reckon?' said the director, who was a cheerful sort of character. 'I think it's going all right. Here – look – I like this bit. Where the old girl comes out of the launderette in front of the truck ... '

Ronnie groaned, and hid his face again.

In the *Out For The Count* studio, Alex was getting restless. Something was wrong somewhere. Louise was happy enough, now she'd got all the bubblegum back

114

in her mouth, and the boys were all sitting there like little lambs, waiting to jeer and boo.

The Germans weren't too happy. There'd been two broken collar-bones, a dislocated shoulder, and some bruised ribs after the incident in the corridor, and when the survivors had been sat down in the studio, the warm-up man, who'd got the wrong end of the stick, had upset them all by telling Hitler jokes. There was a lot of muttering and frowning going on.

But it wasn't that which was bothering Alex. He knew they'd come to see *Street Noise*, but this didn't look like the *Street Noise* set. And that guy with the white suit and the lime-green shirt, gabbling to the guy with the headphones in the corner – wasn't that Micky McGee, the man who did quiz shows?

What was going on?

Alex drummed his fingers on his knees and looked around for the exit.

The Delilah film lasted three minutes, which just gave Jacob time to bomb over and have a final word with Gobbo.

On the way, he saw a strange sight: about fifteen horse-freaks standing in a line, with David at the head of the queue, taking money.

'What you doing?' Jacob said.

'Selling Gobbo's autograph,' David told him. 'I thought it was a good idea.'

'How much you charging?'

'Ten p.'

'Make it fifteen,' Jacob told him, and shot off.

David's queue was one of the only two places in the studio where the weenies were under control. The other place was where Nings had got a crowd of them in a corner, terrorised by *the teeth*. Apart from those two islands of calm, they were everywhere: underneath the

115

cameras, swinging on the chairs, climbing on Jumpin'
Joe's piano ... Wherever you looked, there was a small
crawling life-form.

As for Miss Cynthia Pym, Jumpin' Joe had got her
in a corner somewhere sharing his bottle of whisky and
talking about horse-racing. Jacob reckoned Jumpin' Joe
was safe there for a few minutes, unless they got
through the whisky, in which case he'd have to send
Nings up for some more. But that would mean an
immediate increase in the weeny-count. H'mm. Never
mind that for the moment. Where was Gobbo?

Yes, where was he?

Serenata was there in her place, but Gobbo's chair
was empty.

Jacob grabbed Laurie, who was passing.

'How much time is there left on the film?' he said.

Laurie checked his watch and listened to something
on his headphones.

'Fifty seconds,' he said.

'Where's Gobbo?'

'Search me. He was here a minute ago.'

'Where's he gone?' Jacob said to Serenata.

She looked up from her *Journal of Molecular Biology*.
She was the most beautiful girl Jacob had ever seen. She
looked a bit like Sade and a bit like Madonna, but
mainly she just looked stupefying.

'Who?' she said.

'Gobbo! Where is he?'

'Oh yeah. He went to the toilet.'

'*Again*? That's about the twentieth time!'

'Well, he's nervous,' said Serenata. 'It's a well-known
physiological reaction. Besides, he had fifteen Cokes
earlier on, he told me.'

'Great piddling lummock,' Jacob said passionately.
'What we going to do if he doesn't get back in time? We
got – how long, Laurie?'

116

'Thirty seconds.'

Jacob looked around. Seething weenies everywhere, but not a Gobbo in sight ... He could feel himself going insane.

Serenata was saying something.

'What? What? What?' he said.

'I said I'll just have to interview you instead,' she told him, and smiled.

It was the smile that did it. His knees got all weak, and he felt himself blushing like a lighthouse, and then Laurie shoved him into the empty chair.

'Twenty seconds,' he said. 'We'll get Deirdre on Camera One and she can cue you in.'

He bombed off to Deirdre, leaving Jacob helpless.

'Remember,' Serenata told him, 'it isn't cool to panic.'

'I'm not panicking!' Jacob said. 'This ain't panic. This is terror.'

'What do you want to be asked about? The same as Gobbo, or something different?'

'Oh yeah. Right. Well, it's a sensational discovery – a top secret. Where all the styles come from. Ask me about that, okay. Maybe it's best if Gobbo ain't here after all.'

'I don't think he was quite sure about the answers anyway,' she said.

'He *looks* cool, though,' Jacob said.

'Oh, he looks wonderful,' she agreed. 'So do you.'

She smiled, and Jacob felt his insides turn over again.

Through a mist he heard Deirdre doing the introduction.

'Okay,' she was saying, 'that's how Delilah broke her leg. She's in hospital now, and if you want to send her some flowers, don't bother. She gave us a right mouthful when she fell off. Anybody'd think it was our fault, the way she was going on. Still, that's enough of

117

her. Now we got something much more important. We have a guest interviewer this week – the famous, the lovely, the incredible Serenata!'

Serenata was well cool. She looked straight at the camera and said, 'Did you ever wonder where all the styles come from? Why every bloke below the age of twenty-five suddenly started wearing white socks a few years ago, for instance? Well, I'm a model. It's my job to wear the latest fashions, and I thought they were just made up by the designers and copied by the kids on the streets. But apparently it's not like that at all. There's something much more sinister going on. Here to tell us about it is none other than Gaf. How did you make this sensational discovery, Gaf?'

'Right,' he said. 'Hello, viewers. Well, it all started in the subway, where I saw this kid doing a graffiti ... '

Something odd was happening at the other side of the studio. Lou Craggs was standing in front of a camera, talking to it.

'Hi,' he said. 'My name's Lou Craggs. I'd like to tell you about my new movie. I think you'll enjoy it. I play a guy called Ricardo Montez, and I fly this beat-up old Dakota round northern Mexico – it's a Steven Spielberg film, by the way – and one day, I discover ... Say,' he said to the cameraman, 'is this camera live?'

'No,' said the cameraman.

Lou Craggs said something rude, and stalked off to find another camera.

Out For The Count was going nicely. The producer had started to breathe again. There'd been a few nasty moments at the start, but these Germans were joining in all right, and the kids were as good as gold. Micky McGee had got four of them up there now – two Germans, two kids – playing the Name-a-song-in-ten-seconds-or-

118

get-a-bucket-of-cold-water-down-your-neck game, and it was a great success.

As a roar of laughter and applause greeted the latest wrong answer and bucket of water, Alex said to Louise: 'I'm just going out a moment. I don't think this is the right place.'

She didn't hear him, so he left.

In the corridor, he looked in both directions. The only thing he saw was a giant tomato tiptoeing away in the distance, so he followed that, and found himself on the floor below – where he had a shock.

Sidling along, white-faced, was a figure he recognised from a set of photographs.

'Gobbo!' he said, before he could stop himself.

Gobbo looked at him. Alex didn't know whether to do him straight away or not, but Gobbo just nodded.

'Yeah,' he said in a trembling whisper. 'You looking for the show?'

'Yeah,' said Alex, unable to believe his luck. 'Has it started?'

'It's about half-way through,' said Gobbo. 'I gotta go on in a minute.'

'Where is it?'

'In here,' Gobbo told him, pointing to the door. 'Just go in and sit anywhere you want.'

'Right,' said Alex. 'I'll just go and get the squa – my girl friend. Be back in a minute, Gobbo!'

He shot away.

I wonder who that was, Gobbo thought. Must be one of my fans. Have I got time to go again?

'And what about punk, though?' Serenata was saying. 'I thought that was something the kids invented themselves. You're not saying the National Cool Board thought that up as well?'

'You bet they did,' Jacob told her and fifteen million

viewers. 'They worked it all out. They made millions of safety pins and they trained the cool agents for months and months in the gobbing gallery and the spitting range and they had chemists working on spot-developing cream and tooth-rot paste and all sorts. Then they sent out the agents, and within six months everyone in the country was punking about like mad. And it was all organized by a bunch of old men in suits, the whole thing, from start to finish.'

'Well, that's amazing,' Serenata said. 'But what are you going to – '

She stopped then, because someone was edging in front of the camera.

'Hi there,' he said to it. 'This is Lou Craggs. I'd like to talk to you about my new movie. You'll enjoy it. It's called – '

'Oy!' Jacob said. 'Get lost!'

'What's going on?' said Serenata.

'Hi,' said Lou Craggs, giving her a flashing smile. 'My name's Lou Craggs. I've come here to tell you about my – '

'Go away,' Serenata said. 'If I want to hear about your crummy film. I'll ask. This is much more important. Now get out the way – I'm talking to Gaf.'

Stunned, Lou Craggs tottered out of the picture.

'Right,' Jacob went on, 'where was I? Oh, yeah, Well, what we got to do, right ... '

The studio door opened quietly, and the tomato-man crept in. Actually he crept halfway in and then got stuck, but by jumping up and down a few times he freed himself and tumbled inside.

It was pretty chaotic in here, he thought, but at least that maniac in the wallaby-suit was nowhere in sight. The man was off his head. As well as being a terrible actor, he was literally insane. What Gloria could see in him he had no idea.

Still, he could hide in here for a while till they came and took the wallaby-man away. There was a huge packing-case over there – that would do.

He tiptoed over quietly to Winston's box. He couldn't actually sit down, of course, but he leant against it and breathed deeply.

Peace and quiet at last, he thought.

Out For The Count was coming to a climax. There was a team of four Detrendifiers playing against four ex-grocers from Dunkelhausen-am-Weser, and they had to take turns to sit in front of a giant catapult while the rest of their team had ten seconds to answer a question. If they got it wrong, the catapult bombarded the victim with custard pies. Since the Dunkelhausen-am-Weser over-sixties couldn't speak much English and the Detrendifiers had brains full of cartilage and gristle, neither team had had any success with the questions so far.

The audience was loving it.

So when Alex burst in and yelled 'I found 'em, lads!' he was met with a universal groan.

'Oh, come on, Alex,' said one of the squad, 'let's just watch this bit ... '

Micky McGee was asking the German team to add together ten and three, and they were going '*Ho ho ho! Es ist schwierig!*' A dim girl in a swimsuit was standing by the catapult, grinning vacantly. Then a gong sounded and she pulled the lever and fifteen custard-pies flew through the air and covered the old guy in the chair with gunge.

The audience roared with laughter, but Alex was made of sterner stuff. He waded in and grabbed the nearest Detrendifiers, slinging them out towards the door, and when the rest of them saw that he meant business, they quickly scuttled out after them.

'You coming or staying?' Alex said to Louise.

'*Ohhhh*,' she moaned, and flopped up out of the seat.

Micky McGee and the rest of the audience watched in surprise as Alex bustled his squad through the door and away.

'Come on,' they heard him say. 'It's just along here. We got 'em now!'

The only Detrendifiers left were the ones playing the catapult game, and they couldn't understand it at all.

Then one of them spoke.

'I got the answer, lads!' he said. 'It's fourteen! Can I go in the chair next?'

Serenata's interview with Jacob was just coming to an end. Fifteen million kids up and down the country were looking at their favourite styles with horror. Could it be true?

As Jacob wound up by telling them that the mighty Gobbo would be along in a minute to show them some real anti-Cool Board styles, the door of the studio opened quietly, and the wallaby-man looked in.

He wanted to inspect the damage to his rear end before going on with the chase. He'd catch that buffoon in the tomato-suit and drag him kicking and screaming back to Gloria (and what could she see in *him*, for Heaven's sake?). But first he wanted to check the state of his costume. Ever since that brush with the German mob in the corridor, he'd been conscious of a strong draught around his backside, and he had the uncomfortable feeling that he wasn't as well covered up as he might be.

Now, where could he go?

That big box over there with the ropes around it – he could hide behind that and peer at himself. He crept towards it carefully.

Deirdre and Julie were conferring busily. Julie had Gobbo pinned down in a chair, and she was adjusting his hair and straightening his collar.

'It's no good expecting him to speak,' she said to Deirdre. 'Look at him!'

Gobbo was pale and still and seemed to be hypnotised by terror.

'He doesn't hardly know where he is, poor thing,' Julie went on. 'It's stage-fright.'

'Well, he's just *got* to go on,' Deirdre said. 'We got the whole show building up to Gobbo, and if he doesn't come on, we're going to be well shamed up ... Wait a minute, what's his hand doing?'

Gobbo's right hand was making strange little chopping movements.

'Oh, that's his karate,' Julie explained. 'He's gone into a trance, I expect.'

'Hang on! I got an idea. Don't let him move!' Deirdre said, and belted away to find Laurie.

She just had time to explain what she wanted before going and dragging Jumpin' Joe King away from Miss Cynthia Pym.

'Get to the piano!' she hissed at him. 'You're on next!'

A bunch of fascinated weenies followed him as Deirdre turned to the camera. Jacob's interview with Serenata was just over.

'Okay, viewers,' Deirdre said, 'you know what to do now, right? You got to check all the cool very carefully just in case it comes from the Cool Board. But now we got something decent. We only met this old geezer today, but he's a right laugh. He's had a bottle of whisky already, so he's well tanked up, but he's genuine cool all right. In fact he was being cool before my dad was born. Here he is – Jumpin' Joe King!'

Jumpin' Joe King was a skinny old black American guy with a baggy suit and a bow tie. When he saw the camera was on him, he held up the bottle of whisky with a crafty expression.

'This whisky's half-full of air,' he said. 'It's a damn shame. I'm going to play the piano now. I been playing the piano for forty years, and I ain't won yet. Okay.

Here goes with the Air-In-The-Whisky-National-Cool-Board Blues. Stand back. Git ready. Here she comes.'

He put the bottle down and started belting away at the piano. You could tell he'd been playing it for forty years; he certainly seemed to know where all the notes were. He was playing about twenty at once, and his right foot was pounding up and down to keep the beat in order. Then he started to sing.

> *'Oop bop sh'bam*
> *Sh'diddly up a teen a rooni*
> *Klook a been a mop mop*
> *A wah wah wah.'*

Then his left hand chased itself up and down the keyboard while his right hand lifted the bottle back to his lips.

'The different parts of my body,' he explained to the camera, 'have achieved a high degree of mutual independence. For example, behold the following.'

He put the bottle down again, and while his left hand kept on boogieing away, his right hand played the first theme from Tchaikovsky's Piano Concerto No.1.

'Enough to bring tears to the eyes of a meatball,' said Jumpin' Joe. 'I can also smoke while drinking, read the racing page while taking a crap, and sing *Hail To The Chief* while sitting in a bowl of jelly with a naked lady balanced precariously upon my shoulders. All thanks to the independence of the individual parts, only achieved after a lifetime's dedicated practice, and the frequent

124

application of whisky.'

He was still playing away while he said all that. Dozens of gaping weenies were assembling in the darkness behind him, amazed by what he was saying.

'Okay,' he went on, 'now listen. You listening?'

'Yeah!' screamed the weenies.

'You wanna know how to be cool?'

'*Yeah!*'

'Well, you pin back your ears and pay attention. You got 'em pinned?'

'*YEAH!*'

'Okay. Here we go.'

He gave a great flourish on the keys, and then started to sing:

> '*Now I'm going to tell you How To Be Cool*
> *It ain't nothing like what you learn in school*
> *You don't get no cool from magazines*
> *Or the radio or the TV screen*
> *And whatever the Cool Board tries to say*
> *You don't get cool the Cool Board way . . .* '

Everything was calm.

The weenies were all listening to Jumpin' Joe, hoping to hear some rude words; the tomato-man was leaning peacefully against one side of Winston's box, while the wallaby-man was hopping round in tiny circles on the other, trying to see whether his rear end was totally bare; Winston was praying; Julie was whispering urgently to Gobbo; Deirdre was explaining something to Jacob; Serenata was reading her *Journal of Molecular Biology*; the director was tapping his fingers in time to Jumpin' Joe, and watching the cloud of smoke that showed where Ronnie Larkin was sitting. Every so often it swirled and parted and a trembling hand came out to fumble for another cigarette.

'All right, Ronnie?' he said.

'Mumble mumble mumble,' came the reply from the cloud.

'Oh, fair enough,' said the director. 'Where'd you find this old guy? He's pretty good.'

Jumpin' Joe's song came to an end, to a lot of cheering and clapping from the weenies.

Gobbo was in position.

Laurie gave Jacob a signal, and Jacob said to the nearest camera: 'Right. That was Jumpin' Joe King. Brilliant. Now, it's nearly twenty-four and a half minutes since we last saw Winston, and has he got out yet? No, he ain't!'

The camera showed a close-up of Winston's little window, with Winston inside it, mouthing strange words.

'But help is at hand,' Jacob went on. 'Knowing that Winston probably wouldn't manage it, we got the mighty Gobbo to help. And here he is, ladies and gentlemen – the mighty Gobbo in person!'

The camera cut back to show Gobbo. Julie had really worked hard on him. He was wearing a yellow bow tie, a dark blue shirt, narrow blue corduroy trousers and the famous desert boots. He looked stunning. Actually he looked stunned as well; he looked as rigid and pale as a dummy in a shop window. Jacob didn't like the look of it at all.

'Gobbo will now karate the box,' he said loudly, 'and release Winston!'

Nothing happened.

All over the studio, people were holding their breath. Even the weenies were quiet.

Julie whispered 'Go on, Gobbo! You can do it!'

Seconds ticked by ...

And then the studio door burst open and a mob of Detrendifiers poured in.

'Get 'em, lads!' yelled Alex.

That was what did it.

Alex's words bounced around in Gobbo's head, like a ball on a pin-table, until they hit the right spot and lit his tiny brain up.

With a mighty cry, he leapt at the box. One huge blow split the lid open, and then he seized the ropes and snapped them like cotton. He tore the chain off, and the padlock went flying across the studio and whanged a Detrendifier on the knee; and then Gobbo waded in to the rest of the box, hands and feet and head all going, till it was nothing but a heap of splinters, with a trembling Winston in the middle.

He stopped then, a bit dazed, and a cheer rang out. Waves of applause echoed through the studio, and everyone turned to see where it was coming from.

To Jacob's amazement, it was the Detrendifiers.

'Master! Great one!' they were saying to Gobbo, and within seconds he was surrounded by dozens of them, all thumping him on the back and trying to shake his hand.

The director got it all. He also got Alex banging his head on the floor, Louise covered in bubble gum again, and the scene that took place by the smashed-up box.

Because when Gobbo had been carried away in triumph, the wallaby-man and the tomato-man finally saw each other across the splintered ruins.

'Got you at last!' the wallaby-man yelled, and sprang.

The tomato-man didn't have time to waddle away, and the two of them rolled over and over among the splinters, surrounded by cheering weenies and revealing fascinating glimpses of bare flesh. Strange cries came from them – 'Can't act, eh?' 'I'll tell Gloria about – ' 'You great red ba – '

And then the weight fell on them.

'Well, it's only made of cardboard,' Jacob said hotly three minutes later. 'What they making such a fuss for?'

He'd just signed the show off, and the place was in uproar. The wallaby-man and the tomato-man were being carried out, groaning and cursing; David had a line of Detrendifiers in front of him, queueing up for Gobbo's autograph at 50p a time, while Julie and Deirdre were busy turning the autographs out; Gobbo couldn't actually do them himself, because his hands hurt, but Serenata was bandaging them, and he was blushing like a turnip lantern; and in a corner, Nings was explaining to some more Detrendifiers how he got *the teeth*, and watching critically as one after another they hurled themselves face first on to the floor, trying to copy the effect.

But the weenies were everywhere. They were hysterical with excitement, and Miss Cynthia Pym, not having had as much practice with whisky as Jumpin' Joe King, was pie-eyed in a corner. Laurie was going mad.

'We've got to get rid of 'em, Gaf!' he said. 'As soon as I grab one of 'em, three more appear! What do we *do*?'

'All right, leave it to me,' said Jacob, thinking: pitiful. The man can't cope.

He jumped on a chair and yelled '*SHUDDUP!*'

Silence. Everyone turned to look.

'Who'd like a present?' he shouted.

'Me! Me! Me!'

'Well, there's a nice man downstairs who's got a present for every one of you. Go down the stairs and out the front door and – '

He didn't have to finish. They all streamed out like bathwater. Several Detrendifiers went, too.

'Smart move,' said Laurie. 'But what are they going to do when they get there and find there isn't a nice man with presents?'

'I dunno,' said Jacob. 'But if you lock the doors, they won't be able to do it in here, will they?'

Lou Craggs had had enough. They were all crazy in there. He was feeling a little crazy himself by this time; it was as if he'd become invisible or something. He thought that if he didn't manage to tell someone about his film, he'd have to be carried away in an ambulance. Where was everyone? These corridors . . . They went on for ever. They could drive you insane.

He wandered on.

The survivors from Dunkelhausen-am-Weser were limping down the corridor on their way out. The show had been quite amusing, but they were feeling their age by now, not to mention their bruises. All they wanted to do was get to their coach and go back to the hotel for several drinks; they were in no mood for conversation. A big handsome man like a film-star tried to stop them and tell them something, but they shook their heads and walked on.

Just as they got to the front door, they heard a terrifying sound.

They turned – but it was too late. A screeching mob of miniature show-jumpers was hurtling towards them. For the third time that night, the over-sixties club of Dunkelhausen-am-Weser was scattered in all directions, as the crazed weenies hit them like a hurricane and poured on out of the front door to look for the nice man with the presents.

In the shocked silence that followed, someone began to sob.

Miss Cynthia Pym was having trouble with the stairs. Sometimes they went up, and sometimes they went down, and sometimes they did both at the same time.

Something was wrong somewhere. Was it the whisky?

Or was it those thirty or forty ancient foreigners draped across the fittings like extras in the cemetery scene from a video nasty?

She couldn't really take it in. And then someone tapped her on the shoulder, and she turned blearily to find a strange man grinning at her.

'Hi,' he said. 'Let me introduce myself. My name's Lou Craggs, and I'd like to tell you about my new movie. It's called – '

It was all too much. Miss Pym leaned forward suddenly and was violently sick.

Lou Craggs found the front door and stumbled out into the car-park. He found a railing and gripped it convulsively, fearing for his reason, and closed his eyes and breathed deeply three or four times.

'*There he is!*'

A shrill voice rose into the air, and Lou Craggs turned in horror to see a frenzied mob bearing down on him – boot – helmets – whips – strange cries –

'*The man with the presents!*'

With a wild yell, he turned and made off into the night.

The last of the Detrendifiers had been rounded up and thrown out. Peace was returning to the studio.

The director pushed the script away and sat back.

'Well done, Ron,' he said. 'Nice little show. Bit hairy at times, but the punters'll like it. When that weight fell down ... Ronnie? What's the trouble?'

Ronnie Larkin was sitting there rigid, his eyes glazed, five cigarettes between his fingers. The assistant director prodded him, but he didn't move.

'Leave him,' said the director. 'He'll wake up when the fags burn down. Let's go and have a drink. If there's any whisky left ... '

13

GLITTERING BLIPS

Next morning, How To Be Cool woke up to find themselves famous.

It was Jacob's interview with Serenata that really did it. Every kid who'd heard the show was struck with a terrible suspicion: were all their styles really thought up by a bunch of old creeps in suits? Was nothing safe? *Yeeeuuuuugggghhhh*!

The TV company was besieged by phone calls for How To Be Cool; disc jockeys blew the dust off a load of old Jumpin' Joe King records; the yellow-sock-and-suede-boot count went up by a thousand per cent; and on Monday morning at school, Jacob saw at least six kids with their hands in plaster and bandages on their heads.

Gobbo felt bad about that.

'You shouldn't have let me do it, Gaf,' he said, after the last kid had come up to have his plaster autographed. 'You need proper training before you can karate things. You gotta be in a trance and that. I don't like to think of all them kids hurting themselves.'

'Don't be ridiculous,' said Jacob. 'If you hadn't done that we'd have been well shamed up. Anyway, if these kids ain't got the sense to see it's going to hurt whanging their hands against great packing cases, they wouldn't take any notice even if you had a health warning stencilled all over your bum, like that kangaroo.'

He wasn't quite sure what he meant by that, but it was all the same to Gobbo. Jacob was a bit preoccupied. It was all very well having a hundred weenies gaping at them in wonder, but the silence from the Cool Board was ominous. And Henry hadn't turned up at the Rec, either. Jacob needed to go off somewhere with Deirdre and work out what to do next, because he had an uneasy feeling, and he didn't know why.

Mr Cashman had an uneasy feeling, too, but he knew precisely where his one came from. Three seconds after the end of *Street Noise*, the phone had rung in his office. His hand trembled as he picked it up.

'This is Downing Street,' said a cold voice at the other end. 'The Prime Minister would like a word with you.'

Mr Cashman automatically stood up, frigid with dread.

'Good evening, Prime Minister,' he said. 'I – '

Gabble gabble gabble, went the phone.

'Yes, Prime Minister. I fully accept that. All the same – '

Yak yak yak, the phone said. *Drone drone yak yak moan moan moan.*

'Yes, straight away, Great One. But I must point out that – '

Gabble gabble YAP!

The phone was slammed down at the other end.

Mr Cashman gulped, and ran a finger around the inside of his collar. What he actually wanted to do was run away and get into a cupboard, but he was a man of decision, so he poured himself a large glass of gin instead. Then he sent for Sylvianne.

'Call all Heads of Department,' he said. 'I want them here. Now. Emergency meeting. At once. All of them. Right away.'

He felt a bit tougher once he'd said that, and

Sylvianne was certainly impressed. She tiptoed away and went to ring up all the Heads of Department, and Mr Cashman brought out his gin from under the desk and took a good long suck at it. It was going to be a heavy meeting.

Someone else was feeling uneasy as well, and that was Prakash. He'd been monitoring the cool waves during *Street Noise*, and they'd gone haywire. At first he thought it was the Coolometer playing up, but after he'd given it a swift belt or two and found that it made no difference, he began to get worried.

As soon as the programme was over he slung his little brother off the computer, where he was playing a game called *Doomsword of Gongolblath*.

'Hey!' said his brother. 'You had it all last week. It's my turn.'

'This is serious,' Prakash said. 'I need it for some calculations. Get lost.'

But he had to promise to buy him another game before his brother would leave him alone. Pretty soon he had graphs and equations of all kinds flickering away, and what he discovered turned his blood cold.

As he'd suspected, cool waves were one of the fundamental forces of the universe. Scientists had reckoned for a long time that these forces were all joined together in some way, and that if you tweaked one of them, all the others jiggled in response.

And with the massive shift in the cool-values of the universe caused by *Street Noise*, anything could happen. Electro-magnetism – gravity – they could all go up the creek. This was seriously alarming.

Prakash spent all Friday evening and most of Saturday at the computer, breaking off only to shoot out and buy his brother the game he'd promised. Then it was back to the screen for the rest of the weekend. By the time he'd finished, glassy-eyed, he'd come to one or two conclusions, but he'd need to rig up the Coolometer for a twenty-four hour cool watch to be sure. Now where could he find a barograph?

His little brother shoved him aside, and settled down with *Stormswallower of Flelthulfroth*.

Mr Staines wasn't uneasy at all. In fact he was tremendously excited. He'd just had a message from the Education Office to say that a high-level civil servant from Whitehall was coming to the school for an indefinite period to look into questions of school management, and he was so delighted that he called a special staff meeting during break.

'I want us all to carry on absolutely as normal,' he said to everyone. 'We must get all the classrooms tidied up. A new display in the entrance – Mrs Blanchard can get some flowers – the Morris Dancing Club can welcome him when he arrives – '

'You realise the kids are all up in the air today?' said the French teacher.

'Are they? Why?'

'This *Street Noise* nonsense,' said the R.E. teacher.

'Noise? In the street? Someone been complaining?'

'It's a programme on television,' someone explained. 'You know what television is?'

'Programme? Are we going to be on television? Marvellous! What is it, a sort of quiz show? We'll arrange a coach trip. Cancel the timetable. I'll see about cheerleaders. Who's picking the team?'

They eventually got it into his skull that most of the kids had seen Jacob and Deirdre and the others on TV, and were all excited about it.

'Something to do with *cool*,' said the Maths teacher. 'I can't understand what they're talking about.'

'The National Cool Board! I know!' said Mr Staines.

'You've just got to keep in touch with them. Talk to them in ways they respond to. *I* know what's going on in today's teen scene. Who's teaching Jacob's class after break?'

'Me,' said the Science teacher. 'Worse luck.'

'Send him to me, would you? And the others, Gombo and the rest. You probably call him Raymond. Oh, I know quite a lot about what's going on, you'd be surprised.'

'I think we all would,' said the Design teacher. 'Tell me, why is this civil servant coming anyway? What have we done to deserve it?'

'Oh, government business,' said Mr Staines vaguely. 'Some sort of inter-departmental exercise. You know what they're like. We must do a good assembly tomorrow – show them what we're capable of.'

'We can't,' said the Deputy Head. 'They're coming to rewire the Hall, remember.'

'So they are. Cancel assembly tomorrow. Carry on absolutely as normal.'

The civil servant whose visit was making Mr Staines so excited was actually nothing of the sort.

Twenty-four hours before, the exhausted, red-eyed Heads of Department at the National Cool Board had run out of ideas. Their emergency meeting had gone on for a day and a half already, and they'd discussed every way they could think up of dealing with the menace of How To Be Cool, and got nowhere.

Then, finally, Lizzie the trouser expert spoke up.

'You've probably thought of this already,' she said, 'but what about infiltrating their school? Send in a secret agent – not the Detrendifiers – someone clever. Disguised as a school inspector or something. Just to find out what they're up to and sort of keep them so busy they can't do anything else till the Cool Board's been sold.'

There was a little silence. No–one wanted to speak before Mr Cashman in case they said the wrong thing.

'At last,' he said. 'I was wondering who'd spot that. Well done, Lizzie. As for the rest of you . . . ' He looked around with bottomless contempt. 'Call yourselves Heads of Department? Pathetic. Well, this is your chance to redeem yourselves. I want a volunteer. This is a dangerous mission . . . '

So it was that on Monday morning, a keen–eyed Cool Board official was bombing keenly along the motorway towards Fen Street School. His name was Parkinson. He was keenly looking forward to the mission. He was so keen, in fact, that no–one liked him at all, not even the rest of the Cool Board. He was just the man for the job.

Mr Cashman, meanwhile, had had another idea. He called in the Chief Security Officer.

'This man Henry,' he said. 'Ex–Research Director.'

He passed a photograph across, and the Chief Security Officer frowned at it through the visor on his crash–helmet.

'Yes, Mr Cashman?' he said.

'He's loose. I'm not sure, but I think he's up to something. I want him brought in.'

'Gaf?'

'What? I'm busy, man. Look at all these Gobbo-graphs we got to do. Kids all over the country want his autograph, and he goes and knackers his hand,' Jacob said bitterly. 'We ought to make him sign 'em with his foot. It wouldn't make much difference, the way he writes. What d'you want, anyway?'

It was breaktime, and Prakash had finally found the others on the wall by the Science room, surrounded by piles of fan mail.

'It's urgent,' he said. 'Look, I been working all weekend at this. It's the waves. They've gone nuts.'

'What you talking about?' said Deirdre.

'Something's happened to the cool waves,' Prakash said. 'They couldn't take the pressure from *Street Noise*. I got this barograph, right, and I hooked it up to the new Coolometer – 'cause I made a new one last week – anyway, it's printing out a record of the general background cool all through the universe. And there's this new pattern. Every eighty minutes there's a definite blip. I never seen nothing like it.'

'What d'you mean, a blip?' said Jacob suspiciously. 'We got enough to do without thinking about blips.'

'What's a barograph, anyway?' said Nings.

'It's a thing, right, it kind of draws a line on a revolving drum. A printer'd be even better, now I think of it. A dot-matrix printer with a ZA32080 interface – '

'Huh,' said Jacob. 'If you go on like this, you're going to end up with blips all over *your* interface. We got work to do. Here – start turning out some of these Gobbo-graphs.'

'No, belt up, Gaf,' said David. 'This is important. What do they mean, these blips?'

'Well, every eighty minutes all the cool goes into reverse for a bit. We probably ain't noticed it yet. But it's getting stronger, that's the point. We got to watch out for any weird changes in what's cool. That'll prove it definitely. The trouble is ... '

'What?' said Deirdre, as the bell went. 'What's the trouble?'

'Well, I don't think there's any way of stopping it. I think we've done something sort of fundamental. It looks as if the cool's out of control.'

That was pretty worrying. As they queued up for Science, they thought about what it might mean.

'We could lose everything,' said Jacob. 'And we only just got started ... '

'So will the Cool Board, though,' Deirdre pointed out. 'There won't be anyone in control.'

'The whole *world's* going to go haywire,' said Jacob nervously. 'That's if it happens like Prakash says. We got to watch out for weird cool fluctuisms.'

'I seen one already,' said David. 'I looked at Nings during assembly, right, and you know what he was doing?'

'Shut up,' said Nings. 'I weren't.'

'What?' said Gobbo.

'He was singing the hymn,' said David.

'I'll do you!' said Nings.

'He looked well cool, and all,' said David, ignoring him. 'I couldn't understand it.'

'McNab was watching me,' said Nings hotly. 'I had to.'

'Yeah, but you were enjoying it,' said David, holding him off.

'Pack it in,' said Jacob, as they went into the lab. 'Now belt up, okay? Just watch for the blips.'

The lesson hadn't begun before the Science teacher sprang a surprise.

'The Head wants to see you,' he said. 'All your trendy little gang, in fact. Go on, push off there now.'

Jacob called a quick meeting by the cloakroom on the way.

'The last time he done this, Mr Cashman was there,' he reminded them. 'We're not doing any deals, right. We got 'em on the run. So whatever he says, we say *no comment*, okay?'

When they got there, they found Mr Staines in the corridor, dealing with a pile of chairs and a teacher.

'No, Suzanne, I won't forget,' he said. 'It's at the forefront of my mind. Solemn promise. Leave it to me.

Now I've got to get on with this – this is *really* important.'

He hustled her away and turned to beam at the kids.

'So!' he said. 'On the telly, eh! Come and take a chair, come on. Let's go in my office and talk about it. We're really making the scene now, eh? Brill!'

'Yeah,' said Jacob.

They each took a chair and trooped heavily into his office. When they were all in, he opened the door into Mrs Blanchard's room and said 'Mary – go and find some orange squash, will you? Oh, and those new biscuits we got for the governors' meeting – bring them as well.'

He shut the door before she could protest, and urged them all to sit down.

'Ah, Balj – Parv – umm,' he said, beaming at Prakash. 'So you're one of the gang, eh. Good-oh. Take a seat, don't be shy. Now, tell me all about it. All right, Debbie?'

'Yeah,' said Deirdre.

'And Gombo, eh! The famous model!'

'I ain't a model,' Gobbo muttered. 'I'm real.'

'Ha, ha! Great! Come on, then, let's hear all about it.'

He sat down with them and hitched up his trousers. He was still wearing his white socks.

'Well, there's not much to tell, really,' Jacob said. 'We just went up and done the show and come back again.'

'Modesty, eh! I bet you were thrilled,' Mr Staines chortled. 'All those cameras and lights and such. What was the programme about?'

'Styles,' Jacob said.

'Styles, eh. And what did you do?'

'We just done interviews and that,' said Deirdre.

The door opened and Mrs Blanchard came in with a tray. There was a jug of weak orange squash on it, and a pile of plastic beakers, and a packet of chocolate biscuits.

'There,' she said, banging it down on Mr Staines's desk, and giving him a look that would have stopped a JCB. 'And when would you like me to go and get some more biscuits for the governors?'

'I think they've got some of these in the staffroom,' said Mr Staines. 'Have a look in Mrs Atkinson's locker – she won't mind.'

'You've got the Maths Adviser coming in at eleven o'clock,' she said. 'I wouldn't like you to miss him, like you did last time.'

'Put him in the library, Mary. I'll see him when I've finished. These people have to learn to wait, you know. I mean, what's a school for?'

'I don't know,' said Mrs Blanchard sourly. 'I've forgotten.'

Jacob and Deirdre exchanged a look as she went out. She looked as if she had more trouble with Mr Staines than they did, even.

Mr Staines was happily pouring out the orange squash, and trying to get Gobbo to say something other than *No Comment*, when something strange happened.

Julie, who was sitting opposite him, suddenly gave a little squeak and said 'I'll help you, Mr Staines!'

She took the packet of biscuits from his hand and tore it open. Half of them fell on the floor.

'Oh, I'm so sorry!' she said, and got down on her knees to pick them up. 'I just went all weak – I couldn't help it, Mr Staines! It was when you looked across at me – I – I – '

The others couldn't believe it. She was blushing and stammering and gazing at him with love and wonder all over her face. She looked like Gobbo watching Manchester United.

'That's all right,' he said. 'Give her a hand, Gombo, that's it. The floor's quite clean!'

Gobbo himself was staring at her with deep suspicion, but she couldn't see that. He got down to help her while Mr Staines turned to Prakash and tried to talk to him.

'What's the matter with you?' Gobbo muttered to Julie.

'I dunno!' she whispered. 'He's just so cool!'

'Eh? Who?'

'Mr Staines ... '

It was too much for Gobbo's brain. When his flimsy little circuits overloaded, a sort of automatic switch cut out all the incoming information for a while, and he sat back peacefully and said 'Oh.' It was Nature's way of being merciful.

'Oh,' he said, sitting back peacefully.

Meanwhile, Mr Staines was trying to understand what Prakash did in the organization.

'Well, I'm an adviser, kind of thing,' said Prakash. He was watching Julie, and trying to see the time. Had eighty minutes gone past since assembly, when Nings had blipped? 'It's nothing special. Kind of technical, really.'

'Very good idea,' said Mr Staines. 'In the multi-cultural field, no doubt. Yes, we're all for that. I expect your friends in the National Cool Board are very interested in that kind of thing. How's Mr Cashman, by the way?'

He was obviously prepared to settle in for the morning. But Jacob was alarmed, and he decided to take charge, which was the only way of dealing with Mr Staines.

He finished his squash and stood up.

'Thank you for the drink, Mr Staines,' he said. 'It's eleven o'clock now, so I expect your visitor'll be waiting. Anyway, we got a Science lesson to go to.'

'Yeah, we don't want to miss Science,' said David.

'Not with Mr McNab demonstrating his crampons. That's a right laugh, that is.'

Mr Staines had a mouthful of biscuit, with another biscuit in one hand and a beaker of orange squash in the other, and there were crumbs all over him. He looked like a big fat disappointed baby with a beard.

They left him there and shot off back to the cloakroom.

'Right,' said Deirdre to Julie. 'What got into you, then?'

'Oh, yeah,' said Gobbo. 'She come over all strange. I remember now.'

Julie was rubbing her forehead and looking puzzled.

'I dunno,' she said. 'I must have been dreaming or summat. It's gone now. Ugghhh, it was weird.'

'What?' said Jacob. 'What happened?'

'I thought Mr Staines was cool,' she said.

There was a moment's shocked silence.

'It's all right now,' she went on. 'By the time we left he'd gone normal again. It just sort of come over me. One minute he was sitting there like a – like a butter mountain, and the next minute he was all glamorous and hunky. It was *uncanny*. It only lasted about a minute and then it went.'

They all looked at each other. This was really serious. Jacob felt the panic starting to bubble like porridge.

'It's a blip!' he said. 'We're all doomed! If *he* can be cool, then – '

'Oh, belt up,' said Deirdre. 'Stop panicking and think. Prakash – are you sure about the waves?'

'Dead certain,' he said. 'It happened exactly eighty minutes after the hymn in assembly. And like I said, it's getting stronger.'

'Right,' said Jacob sternly. 'Well, you're in charge of the waves. You get 'em sorted out. We can't go on like this.'

At the same time, while the Maths Adviser who'd come to see Mr Staines was drumming his fingers on the library table and looking at his watch, Mr Staines was showing a keen-eyed visitor into his office. He had a dark suit, dark Brylcreemed hair, shiny black shoes and a shiny black briefcase. Mr Parkinson had arrived.

When Jacob and the others got to the Rec that afternoon, Henry was still missing. Sitting on the bench ahead of him there was a thin droopy-looking girl with long dark hair and a notebook.

She looked up when she saw them and said 'Jacob? Is that you?'

'Yeah,' he said. 'But no interviews, right. We can do you an autograph if you want, but – '

'Hang on,' said Deirdre, 'aren't you Sandra? Henry's girlfriend?'

'Yes,' she whispered, and her eyes got all moist. 'They've taken him prisoner . . . '

'*What*?'

Jacob was interested straight away. The others clustered round open-mouthed to listen.

'What happened?' said Deirdre. 'Where've they got him?'

'I don't know,' she said in a shaky voice. 'Three men in crash helmets came to his boarding house yesterday and took him away in a big van. I think they must be Security Guards from the Cool Board – unless he's an international terrorist, I suppose . . . D'you think he could be an international terrorist?'

'No,' everyone said at once.

'Nor do I. I think he'd've told me. We used to share everything, Henry and I. I read him all my poems. I was just writing this one when you came along – it's about him, actually. It's called "Three Ducks and Me", and – '

'Yeah, decent,' said Jacob. 'Sounds brilliant. But why would they take him prisoner? Didn't he leave any message?'

She shook her head. 'They took him so quickly – great big men they were, his landlady said. With ever such fat legs.' Her voice got dangerously wobbly, and Jacob took a step backwards in case she started to cry. 'I don't know what to *do*!'

'They'll probably torture him,' Jacob said helpfully. 'I saw this film, right, and – '

'Waaaaah!' she went, and Deirdre turned to Jacob and gave him a scornful look.

'Don't be stupid,' she said. 'Just go and play on the swings or something while I sort this out.'

'I was only trying to help,' he said. 'I mean, they might come back for her next. And if they torture – '

'*Waaaaaahhhh!*'

'I dunno what's the matter with her,' Jacob grumbled. 'Anyone'd think I was trying to upset her.'

'What we gonna do, Gaf?' said Gobbo.

'Do about what?'

'Well, Henry and that. And the cool waves.'

'Oh, Henry. I suppose we better rescue him. As if we hadn't got enough to sort out. I dunno,' Jacob said bitterly, 'seems to me we've had nothing but hassle right from the start. I'm beginning to think we'd've been better off doing flower arranging.'

'How's the blip-count?' David asked Prakash.

'Steady,' said Prakash. 'I'll have to look at the barograph to make sure, but I think it's holding. We gotta be careful, though. Anything could tip the balance and send it into a vortex.'

'Into a what?' said Nings.

'A vortex. A sort of whirlpool thing, like the water going down the plughole. I ain't done all the equations yet but I think that's what'd happen.'

'And what'd happen then?' said Jacob.

'I dunno. I'm working in the dark,' said Prakash. 'Quasars and black holes ain't nothing beside this. I'm going where no-one's even *thought* of, man. This is the frontier of science.'

That was so impressive that David changed the subject.

'Here,' he said, 'who was that geezer going round with Staines today?'

'Yeah, I saw him,' said Gobbo. 'I reckon he's a spy from the Cool Board. Old Staines brought him in to Maths, right, and he stared at me all the time.'

'I reckon he never saw anything like you before, Gob,' said Nings.

'No,' Gobbo agreed. 'Probably not. He's bound to be from the Cool Board, 'cause – '

'Here, she's finished,' Jacob said.

Sandra was drifting away with her notebook, and Deirdre and Julie came over to the swings.

'Well?' he asked.

'We had to listen to "Three Ducks and Me",' Deirdre said. 'It was terrible.'

'Well, that's your fault. Didn't she say anything useful?'

'She didn't have much more to say,' Deirdre said. 'But she's going to keep her eyes open at the Cool Board and come back here tomorrow. You never know, she might find out something useful.'

'Here, Gaf,' said David. 'What we going to do next? We got to keep up the pressure on the Cool Board.'

'Yeah, we can't let it slack up now,' said Nings. 'That'd be well bad.'

'Don't panic,' said Jacob. 'I got it all sorted out. I'm just putting the final touches to the final plan. I'll tell you what it is tomorrow.'

He refused to say any more, mainly because he

hadn't got a plan at all. He just hoped he'd have one by the morning.

When he got back home, he heard weird noises coming out of Louise's room. He'd hardly seen her since *Street Noise*; she'd come back on her own and just slunk into her bedroom and said nothing to anyone.

H'mm, he thought. He crept up to the door and listened carefully. The noises were even weirder when he got close up to them. At first he couldn't work it out at all, but then he realised that she was singing along with a record. What made it even stranger was that it was a Barry Manilow record.

Well, she'd finally flipped, he thought. Shaking his head sadly, he went away to do his homework. He reckoned he'd have to spend maybe four and a half minutes on it tonight, because he was well behind in French. Still, you had to work if you wanted to get on.

Actually, Louise hadn't gone mad. She'd decided that she was too sophisticated for the likes of Alex; she was getting bored with *Top of the Pops* and bubble gum anyway. The Barry Manilow record was a sign of her new sophistication, and she didn't care who knew it.

Her taste was maturing in all kinds of ways, she reckoned. She'd noticed it for some time. She was listening to Radio Two a lot these days, for the intellectual stimulus, and what's more, the quality of her fantasies had gone up.

Her main fantasy was sensational. She'd had it for a while now, and it was top secret. She'd fallen in love with the Duke of York.

Only she never thought of him as the Duke of York. She'd seen a picture of him in the *TV Times* before he was married, and she'd realised straight away that here was the man for her. There was something awesome

146

about him – a combination of brutal hunkishness with the delicate shyness of a lost fawn – which melted her brain at once, so she slung out her pictures of Paul Young and Andrew Ridgley and all the other has-beens and stuck him up instead.

On the day of the Royal Wedding, she thought her heart would break. She stayed up in her room, sulking and snarling, till it was all over, and then went out for a long walk to decide what to do with the rest of her ruined life.

Being Louise, she couldn't decide anything, and in any case she met Amy on the way and they went for a hamburger instead; so she just pretended it hadn't happened. No Sarah Ferguson – no wedding – no Duke of York. As far as Louise was concerned, he was still Prince Andrew, and he always would be; and someday, she reckoned, if she hung about town looking her loveliest, a big car would draw up with him in it, and . . .

The fantasy got a bit hazy there, apart from a couple of sensational bits involving a helicopter, but all in all, Louise was doing very well, thanks.

Later that evening, a meeting took place at the edge of the city.

Alex and the Detrendifiers had been sacked by Mr Cashman, and it hurt. All that skill! All that dedication, thrown away like an empty Cheepicola can!

But Alex was a pretty hard nut, and he was determined to fight back. So at nine o'clock he and half a dozen of the knobbliest Detrendifiers met in the cafeteria at the Travellers Tum to plan what they should do next.

'We could set up another Cool Board, kind of thing,' said one. 'Like cause we kind of know the ropes, right.'

'We oughter smash 'em,' said another. 'Both lots.'

147

'No,' said a third one. 'What we oughter do, right, we oughter go and join How To Be Cool. I been practising on this old tea chest indoors,' he added proudly.

He looked it, too. He was covered in plaster and bandages; you could only see one eye, and that was black and bloodshot.

Alex shook his head impatiently.

'That's your trouble,' he said. 'You got no patience, you got no craft, you got no supplety. Now I happen to know how these How To Be Cool kids got so much power. You seen the papers? You listened to the radio since *Street Noise*, have you?'

They nodded. The media were delighted to have some new styles to talk about, and now that the Cool Board was out in the open, the politicians could have a go at it too. The papers had started taking sides; questions had been tabled in the House of Commons; everyone was getting in on it. There was no doubt about it, How To Be Cool had made a big impact. And if Alex knew how they'd done it . . .

The Detrendifiers shuffled closer to listen. Their little eyes were frowning with concentration.

'This guy Jacob,' said Alex. 'His sister Louise told me they've got a machine. It's dead secret, that's why they didn't show it on *Street Noise*. Well, this machine, right, it sends out cool rays.'

He paused to let this drill down through the protective layers of cartilage. When he guessed it had reached their brains, he went on:

'What they do, they stick anything they want in front of the machine, and turn it on, and the rays come out and make it cool, see. So – '

'We could nick it!' said a Detrendifier.

'Good boy,' said Alex. 'Well done. You can have a doughnut.'

'Oh, ta, Alex,' said the Detrendifier, blushing, and went off to buy one.

'Right, we gotta nick it,' Alex went on. 'Once we got control of the cool rays, we can do what we like. We can sell it to Mr Cashman, we can set up another cool board, we can hire ourselves out as cool consultants – anything we like. What about that, then?'

Awe and wonder were written all over their faces. Then the other Detrendifier came back with his doughnut. Alex helped himself to it.

'Here!' said the Detrendifier, hurt. 'You said I could –'

'Yeah, and now I'm fining you one doughnut for interrupting,' Alex told him. 'We gotta have discipline in this outfit. We gotta have *obedience*.'

He jammed the doughnut into his mouth and scowled. All the Detrendifiers waited respectfully till he could speak again, and then listened as he told them what to do.

Jacob lay awake.

Yet again he had to think of something cool; yet again he had to come up with a stunning new scheme that would knock the Cool Board sideways. It wasn't easy. And now it was half-past midnight, and Mouldy the dog was howling like a werewolf in the kitchen, and his dad was stomping around cursing, and Louise's Barry Manilow records were droning away through the wall, and Mr Cashman ... and Gobbo ... and Deirdre ... and Mr Staines ... and the cool waves ... and Henry ... and yellow socks ... and the blips ... and ... and Barry Manilow ... and ...

Round and round it all went.

Just before three o'clock, he had an idea, and thirty seconds later he fell asleep. About time too, he thought.

As well as Jacob's brain, there were two other major centres of activity during the small hours.

One was a locked room in the heart of the Cool Board, where Henry was being tortured.

Actually, they weren't torturing him very much. They just let him think that if he didn't confess, a Security Guard would come in and remove his nose with a pair of pliers.

That being the case, he confessed to everything he could think of. He confessed so much that they had to ask him to stop, and bring a word-processor in to try and keep track of it all. Teams of interrogators and typists worked feverishly through the night, as Henry's disordered imagination went into hyper-drive.

The other centre of activity was Prakash's back garden. All the houses in the terrace backed on to a narrow lane behind some garages, and at about two o'clock a battered van drew up there and some shadowy figures got out.

'Which one is it, Alex?' whispered one.

'This one. With the shed,' said another. 'That's where it is. Now get a move on ... '

In the near-total darkness, the shadowy figures clambered over the fence, stumbled along the path, fumbled with the door of the shed, and after several minutes of stubbed toes and scraped hands and muffled curses and torn jeans, they lugged the Mark I Coolometer out of the shed and into the van.

Half an hour later it was standing in Alex's kitchen, with a group of ex-Detrendifiers staring at it, baffled.

'How's it work, Alex?' said one.

'You plug it in, of course,' said Alex scornfully, shoving a plug into the nearest socket.

One flash and puff of smoke later, the Coolometer started to hum and jiggle promisingly. Alex, bandaging his hand, watched with narrow eyes as the ex-

150

Detrendifiers took turns at standing where they thought the rays were coming out. It didn't do much for them, he thought. Still, give it time.

The moment that Alex plugged the Mark I Coolometer in, the Mark II model in Prakash's bedroom registered a sudden, dramatic change in the backgound cool of the universe, and the barograph began to trace a gigantic blipsurge.

It was the radiator-bottle that did it. Since he wasn't using it any more, Prakash hadn't bothered to keep it filled up, and the amplifying effect hit the cool waves and upset the delicate balance of the fundamental forces for good. As Prakash turned over uneasily in his sleep, the entire physical structure of the universe began to unravel.

14

CHARITY BEGINS AT SCHOOL

Tuesday had the makings of an unusual day from the start.

For one thing, the fundamental forces were playing havoc with all kinds of organic materials. The cornflakes in Nings's kitchen, for instance, had welded themselves into an indissoluble lump with a mass equivalent to a small asteroid, and plunged through the floor towards the centre of the earth, leaving a neat packet-shaped hole in the floor.

In Deirdre's house, the eggs were causing trouble. The shells were all right, but the insides seemed to have developed some kind of anti-gravity, and they slung themselves up at the ceiling as soon as they were cracked. Not only that, but they sat up there for hours, swearing and cursing and using terrible language.

In fact, breakfast was quite an exciting meal. Some people didn't notice, though. Louise was still asleep, because her class had the day off school on account of a staff re-training day about some new exams. Henry was having a rest, and so were the interrogators and the typists. Prakash was belting around in a panic, running from the barograph to the computer to the garden shed and back again. Alex and the Detrendifiers were poking and prodding away at the Mark I Coolometer, trying to find out where the rays came from, and burning their fingers and getting little shocks and losing their tempers. Mr Parkinson from the Cool Board was too keen to have breakfast. He was out in his tracksuit, jogging around the by-pass, working out how to keep Mr Staines from following him around and pointing things out.

It was going to be a busy day all round.

In the Central Police Station, Chief Superintendent Briggs was putting the finishing touches to his biggest operation of the year. A new section of motorway was going to be opened that morning, and Chief Superintendent Briggs was in charge of security for the VIP who was going to open it. He'd organized the route and sorted out mounted escorts and inspected the horses and everything, and now came the big moment: he was going to open the envelope and find out who the VIP was going to be. Because of security it had been kept secret even from him till the morning of the opening.

Chief Superintendent Briggs took his Masonic paper-knife and solemnly slit the envelope. He took out a sheet of thick creamy paper and read the name on it, and found himself standing up and saluting automatically.

Holy Moses, he thought. This is the big one, Briggs. There'll be a medal in this all right.

He grabbed his uniform cap and made for the door. Better get down to the town. Nothing like a last-minute check to keep these young constables on their toes. Blimey, he thought again, hitching up his trousers. Swipe me. *Him* ...

In the school hall, Mrs Murdoch was getting her class ready for assembly, which they were presenting that morning. It was all about the BITE Fund.

That was their favourite charity. It looked after lots of old donkeys who'd lost their teeth. The kids were dead keen on it; they'd seen a film about the Donkey Dental Hospital in Herefordshire, they'd done sponsored swims and house-to-house collections, and they'd held a May Fayre and raised £12.32. They got a letter from the National President thanking them for it. She'd sent them a photograph of herself with an ancient donkey called Vic, which they'd pinned up in their classroom. Two little girls had even embroidered a frame for it.

Mrs Murdoch had planned something even bigger for this assembly. She had a friend called Pippa, who ran a sort of drama group called The Big Pixie Theatre Company, and she'd arranged for them to come in every week and work with the kids on an extended piece of improvised drama about the life of a donkey who'd very tragically lost all his teeth. It was pretty hot stuff. They'd made masks and written songs and practised dances and all sorts, and now they were going to perform it for the first time in front of the whole school. It was called 'The Challenge of the Hay'.

A lot hung on this, and not only for the BITE Fund. The Big Pixie Theatre Company were going to make a videotape of it and use it in their application for a grant from the Arts Council, and if they played their cards right they might even make the Edinburgh Festival. Pippa had been up till midnight taping the sound effects they were going to use, and by the time the first kids arrived she was already hard at work setting up the scenery. Mrs Murdoch was bombing around with pins and sheets of music and tambourines, adjusting costumes and getting out music stands. By five to nine they were all set up, with Gerry, the other half of the Big Pixie, operating the video camera. Any minute now, six hundred kids were going to come in and be awed.

Then the bell went. Nothing happened.

It usually took a couple of minutes anyway to get all the classes down into the hall, so nobody panicked at first. But after five minutes had gone by, the kids in the donkey-costumes started fidgeting, and Mrs Murdoch's hands, poised above the piano keys, were getting more and more tense.

Finally the door opened, and Mrs Blanchard came through with a pile of registers.

'Have you got your register, Mrs Murdoch?' She called. 'We need to know the dinner numbers.'

'We're waiting for assembly!' said Mrs Murdoch.

'Oh, there's no assembly this morning,' Mrs Blanchard told them. 'It's been cancelled. They're rewiring the hall.'

'*What*?'

That was Pippa, of The Big Pixie. She was a large and powerful woman, and while Mrs Murdoch left the piano to comfort the distressed performers she confronted Mrs Blanchard like a landslide.

But Mrs Blanchard wasn't worried.

'Weren't you told?' she said. 'It was decided during the staff meeting at break yesterday.'

'But I was on playground duty yesterday!' said Mrs Murdoch helplessly. 'No-one told me about a meeting!'

'They haven't started rewiring yet, have they?' snarled Pippa. 'You could have an assembly perfectly easily. Make 'em wait.'

'*I* couldn't,' said Mrs Blanchard calmly, 'because I've got work to do. You'd better see the Head. He's in his office. Could I have you. dinner numbers, Mrs Murdoch?'

While Mrs Murdoch, on the verge of tears, counted hands, Pippa stormed off to find the Head. Gerry, who'd seen her at work, opened the nearest door and slipped quietly outside for a smoke.

Mr Staines was just settling down with Mr Parkinson in order to plan their day when the door was flung open and Pippa came bursting in. Mr Staines looked up genially.

'Hello, Miss Potts,' he said. 'What can I – '

'You promised me an audience!' she said.

Mr Parkinson looked up with interest. Mr Staines was puzzled.

'You don't need an audience,' he said. 'Just pop in and

see me any time. My door's always open.'

'In the hall! An assembly!' said Pippa, sounding dangerous. 'Where are they? It was part of the deal, remember? The Big Pixie would come and give our professional expertise for several weeks if you provided a lot of bums on seats for us to videotape. Well, where are they?'

Mr Pakinson was baffled. Mr Staines spread his hands and looked helpless.

'What can I say?' he said. 'It's out of my hands. No-one regrets the effect of this sort of thing as much as I do, believe you me, but what can I do? My hands are tied. I tell you what,' he went on quickly, as Pippa took a deep breath, 'what I can do is this. I can offer the school minibus. Take the cast down to Memorial Square and put the show on there. Involve the whole community. Get the kids out into the real world. The keys are behind Mrs Blanchard's door. Don't worry about the timetable – what's the school for, anyway?'

Pippa didn't bother to answer that. She grabbed the minibus keys from behind the door and set off with a determined gleam in her eyes. Mr Staines turned back to his visitor, who was looking slightly stunned.

'Decision,' he said. 'Prime quality for Headship. Someone has to take the ultimate decisions. Right, what shall we do now?'

The first lesson Jacob's class had that day was Music. Jacob told them all to pay attention for a change, and learn all about crotchets and stuff. It was something to do with his plan, he said. The trouble was that they were all telling one another what had happened at breakfast, and no-one seemed to be interested in his plan. What's more, Prakash was missing.

Just as they were slumping into the Music room, along came Mr Staines with his visitor.

'Hello!' said Mr Staines. 'Music, eh! Swinging! This is

a special visitor called Mr Parkinson. He's come from the Department of Education and Science to have a look at the school. All right, Miss Andrews? I'll leave you to it. Groovy!'

'Here, Gaf,' said Gobbo. 'It's the spy from the Cool Board, look ... '

But Jacob and the others were looking dismayed at the drums and rattles and chime bars lying on the tables. Miss Andrews was a menace. She reckoned she was as good as Andrew Lloyd Webber any day, and she used to write her own songs and make the kids sing them. They were terrible. When they saw all the kit laid out, they guessed they had one of her specials coming, and they were right. She sat Mr Parkinson down in a corner and then gave out some smudgy bits of music paper.

'We've got a new song this week,' she said brightly. 'A friend of mine writes poetry, and I've put one of her poems to music. I'm sure you'll like it. It's called "Three Ducks and Me."'

Jacob and Deirdre and the others felt as if a bucket of cold water had hit them. Sandra? A friend of Miss Andrews'? You didn't think of teachers as having friends, somehow.

Miss Andrews sat down and started tinkling away at the piano. The kids all looked at the words.

'I can't stand it,' whispered Deirdre.

Then something extraordinary happened. All of a sudden the mood of the class changed, and everyone sat up, eager and interested. "Three Ducks and Me" had inexplicably become utterly cool. Only Jacob and Deirdre seemed to be immune. They sat there astonished and open-mouthed as all around them the wimps, the hard nuts and the morons all bellowed away at this appalling rubbish.

'What's going on?' said Jacob.

'It's a giant blip!' said Deirdre, alarmed. 'It's the biggest yet! They're all insane ... Except – hang on –

look at that geezer.'

Mr Parkinson was scribbling furiously in a notebook, and looking all around with a satisfied gleam in his shiny little eyes.

'H'mm,' said Jacob darkly.

The rest of the class, including Gobbo and David and Nings, was roaring out:

> 'Oh, Henry, Henry, Henry,
> How happy I would be
> If you would share my loneliness
> And sit beneath my tree
> With three ducks and me.'

There was clearly something very wrong indeed. Everyone looked as if they thought this was the coolest thing since Gobbo waded into the packing case, and even Jacob felt a strange, primitive desire to start yelling Sandra's terrible words.

With a mighty effort, he controlled it, and held his tambourine in a convulsive grip. He saw Deirdre doing the same with her chime bar. *Bang, bang, rattle, tinkle, clunk*, everyone was going.

> 'My little world is empty
> I look, but I can see
> No Henry by the lonely pond
> A world of miseree
> For three ducks and me.'

Nings was sitting next to Jacob, whacking a cymbal and bellowing with the rest of them. He turned to Jacob and said 'This is decent, Gaf. They oughter make a record of this. That'd be really cool.'

Blimey, thought Jacob, if it's affected Nings, even, it must be deadly.

'What's the matter with you?' he hissed. 'Get a grip

158

on yourself! You're shaming the whole place up.'

Nings looked bewildered, but it did the trick. A wave of sense suddenly came out of nowhere and all the boys faltered and mumbled. Some of the girls carried on, especially the ones who were crying, but most of the class had turned normal again. 'Normal', in music lessons, meant sullen and embarrassed and fed up. Everyone was used to that, so when it came over them again they felt quite comfortable.

'Well?' said Jacob to Nings, under cover of the row.

'I don't know what came over me, man! I just – it seemed to – I can't understand it!'

'I thought you had more control,' said Jacob. 'You sounded a right pillock. "*Three Ducks and Me*",' he said with bottomless contempt.

Nings looked properly ashamed. It was just as well he didn't know how close Jacob had come to joining in.

And Mr Parkinson watched it all with a thoughtful expression.

Meanwhile, Alex and the Detrendifiers were losing patience.

They'd twiddled all the knobs, they'd adjusted all the controls they could find, they'd stood in front of it, behind it, beside it, they'd looked at every dial and stuck their fingers in every aperture, and nothing had happened to make them any cooler. They'd kicked it and sworn at it and burnt their hands, and it just kept on jiggling away to itself and humming quietly, and it was beginning to drive Alex mad.

But then he remembered Louise telling him that Jacob and the others had had it going down in Memorial Square the day they took the pictures for *New Modes*. Maybe it only worked there for some reason. It was worth a try, anyway.

He hitched up his jeans and told the rest of them to load it back in the van. Ignoring the bangs and flashes, the puffs of smoke and the cries of pain, he sat behind the steering wheel, brooding. If all else failed, he could always sell it to Mr Cashman, and watch him get a shock. That'd be good for a laugh.

All this Coolometer-related activity was playing havoc with the fundamental forces of the universe, of course. The food crisis had passed over for the moment, but other materials were feeling the effects. The atomic forces that held rubber together, for instance, had practically given up altogether, with all kinds of disastrous results.

The next lesson for Jacob's class was Maths. Jacob was getting more and more anxious about Prakash.

'Where is he?' he was saying. 'We got giant blips coming at us all the time, and he goes and skives. He's got no sense of responsibility.'

'Yeah, yeah,' said David impatiently. 'Mind out. I got a lot bet on this . . . '

He was backing his faith in the Maths teacher's trousers to the extent of three pounds twenty that morning. There'd been a lot of heavy betting in the corridor outside the classroom, and he was hoping to clean up.

The Maths teacher was bending over to get some books out of his briefcase, and it was clear from the trouser-level that it was going to be an interesting lesson.

But before it could get going, they heard Mr Staines's voice outside in the corridor.

'But you've seen this class already,' he was saying. 'They were doing music. Wouldn't you like to see – '

'No!' said another voice. 'I want to see *this one*!'

Then the door opened, and Mr Staines came in with his visitor, who was looking harassed. He introduced him to the Maths teacher, and then Mr Parkinson went and stood by the door, where he had a good view of Jacob and the others. Mr Staines left, and the Maths teacher turned to the class.

'Right,' he said over the noise, 'thank you, please, that'll do, I said that's enough noise now, come on, get settled, hurry up, no more talking. Now we're going to look at matrices this morning ... '

And he was off. The class settled back, tense and expectant. Jacob reckoned this visitor must be thinking that the teacher was brilliant, to have them all so quiet and attentive. Then he noticed that the visitor was looking straight at him.

H'mm, he thought, and frowned. He took a rubber band out of his pencil case to twang on the table and annoy people. That was usually good for a laugh. But even that didn't work; something had gone wrong with the rubber, and it just stretched and sagged like a piece of Blu-Tack and didn't twang at all.

The teacher droned on and on. Everyone held their breath. Even David got a bit tense.

Then two things happened very quickly.

First, there was a knock on the door and Mrs Blanchard came in.

Second, the visitor's trousers fell down.

That was quite unexpected. No-one knew how to react to that one at all, so they just sat there wide-eyed as Mr Parkinson yelped and bent over and fumbled.

Mrs Blanchard gave him a very curious look.

'I beg your pardon,' she said. 'I was just looking for the minibus keys, but if you're busy – '

Mr Parkinson was still having trouble. The Maths teacher, being a gentleman, decided to help, and picked up his briefcase and held it out to him.

And then *his* trousers fell down, and the class erupted.

Sandra was too upset to go to work that day. The evening before, when her friend the Music teacher had written the tune for 'Three Ducks and Me', she'd been almost overcome. Hearing her words sung made them even more heart-trending, somehow.

One way or another she couldn't face the Cool Board that morning, so she decided to wander along to Memorial Square. She and Henry had shared an ice-cream there once; it had been a wonderful, golden moment. She took her notebook with her in case she thought of a poem. You never knew when you might feel one coming on.

At about that time, Louise was just on the point of waking up. There was no-one else in the house, and she'd been lying there snoring and steaming for hours. It was her cassette player that woke her up. It didn't turn off properly, and the motor had been straining away all night. Finally the tape gave up and snapped, and lashed itself all around the spindles and in and out of the playback head, and the machine lay there howling till Louise woke up and belted it one.

Where am I? she thought. What's the time? What's going on?

The she remembered. No school! Brilliant! And there was no-one else in the house, either.

She scrabbled about under the bed for the fags she kept hidden there among all the fluff, and lit one luxuriously. Prince Andrew was watching from the bedroom wall, so she pushed her pyjama jacket down over one shoulder and made sexy faces at him for a while. Then she got up and slumped downstairs to make some coffee.

Brilliant, she thought. A whole day off. Smart. Decent. Hang on, though ... Hadn't she said she was going to meet Amy at eleven o'clock? There was a new hunk in the sports shop in the precinct, and they were going to try him out. And what was the time now?

Half-past ten. Fair enough.

She slurped up her coffee and lumbered back upstairs to get ready.

There was no point in washing, really. Not really. She was only going to put make-up on again anyway, so why bother?

She started combing her hair. The more she combed it, the more dust came out, so she gave up half-way round. Then she stared in the mirror for about ten minutes. H'mm. Three spots. Maybe if she put some of that orange lipstick on, it might distract attention from them. She fumbled about in the chaos till she found the lipstick, and then did her top lip.

Eeuugghhh, she thought. That's horrible. Where's that white stuff? She rootled around and found it, and carefully did her lower lip in white to see whether it'd be worth doing the top one as well.

When she'd finished, she looked like a tropical fish. But somehow she didn't see that, and somehow she overlooked her spots as well, though two of them were well radioactive. Instead she tried the sexy faces again. Prince Andrew would be pretty impressed, she thought.

She looked at her watch. Blimey! Ten to eleven. She looked around for her clothes.

They weren't there. She snarled. She remembered now; her mum had demanded all her decent things for the wash, since they were starting to ferment, she said. And she certainly wasn't going to wear her school uniform.

What could she do? She looked around crossly. She'd just have to wear her pyjamas, that was all there was to it. They'd really shame her mum up. And there was that cocoa-stain down the front ... Better put a raincoat on, though. They were a bit see-through.

She shoved her feet into her old trainers, grabbed her bubble-gum, and stomped off out.

There were stacks of policemen around that morning, for some reason. Alex couldn't get the van into Memorial Square, so he parked around the corner, and the Detrendifiers piled out and unloaded the Coolometer while he jammed some foreign coins into the parking-ticket machine so he could claim it was broken.

'Here, Alex,' said one of the boys, looking discouraged, 'have we got to take this thing all the way into the square? I burned my hand three times already, and – '

'Do as you're told,' said Alex. 'Ain't you got no pride? Where's your stanima?'

'I dunno,' the Detrendifier mumbled, and picked up his end of the machine.

Memorial Square was unusually busy. As well as all the permanent inhabitants, who were slumped about clutching cans and bottles and beating each other up or being sick, there was a group of buskers at work. Alex wandered up to have a look. They were a pretty professional-looking bunch; there was even a guy with a video-camera shooting them. They had a line of little kids playing musical instruments, and someone in a donkey-costume, and some fat old girl doing a dance; it was impressive.

Suddenly they stopped, and the fat old girl chanted:

'Spring is at an end. Summer comes, and the hay ripens. But it brings no joy to the donkey. He struggles to express his longing ... '

The donkey gave a yell of longing, and a little girl came trotting up with a plastic bowl.

'His owner brings him soup,' said the fat old girl. 'but his heart is too full to eat, so he performs the Warriors' Dance from central Thailand.'

The kids started whacking away at their drums and chime bars, and as the donkey began to lumber up and down Alex moved away thoughtfully. This was high-powered stuff; he wasn't sure if he could compete with it.

164

The boys had the Coolometer set up near a dingy-looking tree. The telly screen was on, and somehow it was picking up an old cowboy programme from the sixties, *Laramie* or *Bonanza* or something. The Detrendifiers, exhausted from their long night, were all gazing at it happily, but they all frowned when Alex came back and pretended they weren't.

He looked at them sadly. He hadn't got the energy to feel cross, somehow.

'You know what,' he told them, 'you're a disappointment to me, you are. I thought I had a good keen squad. I thought I trained you up good. Look at you now. You can't do nothing right. You're just incompinent, the lot of you. Watch your cowboys, go on. I give up.'

He turned his back and wandered to the nearest bench, where he sat down in despair.

At the other end of the bench, clutching her poetry book and hardly daring to move, was Sandra.

Chief Superintendent Briggs was going insane. The fundamental forces of the universe were doing terrible things to his policemen; uniform trousers were shrinking, boot soles melting and sticking to the pavement, and the entire Mounted Escort Division suddenly found themselves riding tricycles.

Reports of new horrors came in every minute. A constable from B Division had to be taken to hospital after being attacked by a hen that turned up from nowhere inside his jacket; five truncheons had grown nastry sets of teeth and bitten their owners in the leg; and the Fire Brigade had to be called out when a constable in Banton Street got trapped under his helmet. It had suddenly grown to the size of a telephone box, and he couldn't lift it up to crawl out.

Then at eleven o'clock came the worst blow of all: a total communications breakdown. All the police radio channels seemed to be occupied by some strange play about a character who couldn't eat properly, and had to go to Herefordshire. He couldn't talk properly, either, by the sound of it. He was in a bad way.

But not such a bad way as Chief Superintendent Briggs. Here he was, on his biggest day of the year, and he'd lost his VIP. Somewhere bombing around the countryside there was a car with *him* in it – and the police had lost him . . .

There was only one thing to be done. Chief Superintendent Briggs sent out the tricycle division with orders to intercept all vehicles on the bypass and escort the right one in to Memorial Square and safety. Otherwise it wouldn't be an OBE he could look forward to; it'd be the Tower of London.

It was break-time.

Jacob, Nings, Deirdre, Gobbo, and Julie sat on the wall by the Science room watching a sort of human avalanche.

Somewhere in the middle of it was David. Dozens of angry voices were yelling things like 'Pay up! You lost! Pay up, man!'

It looked pretty dangerous for him, so they got up and went somewhere else.

Everything was chaotic. Wherever they looked there was total stylistic anarchy. What with the cool waves going wild, and blips coming along every few minutes, anything was cool. Or nothing was. It was impossible to tell. Jacob looked around the playground in despair. There were a hundred different styles on view, and they were all equally cool.

'This is terrible,' he said. 'This is *disgusting*. I mean what's going *on*? This is like a total breakdown of civilization. Where's Prakash?'

'Here, Gaf,' said Nings. 'Look at Gobbo's banana.'

'Eh?' Jacob felt as if his brain was being food-processed. 'What you talking about bananas for? This is

166

a total breakdown of cool, and you go on about bananas – '

'Yeah, but look!'

Gobbo had his lunch box open and was holding out a banana. The fundamental forces had certainly been busy, because it was the first entirely straight banana in the history of the universe.

'I'll swear it was bent when I put it in there this morning,' Gobbo said.

'Well, put it away,' Jacob told him. 'Let's go and find Prakash. How can we concentrate on the cool if we got to waste our time dealing with straight bananas?'

'That's not all, Gaf,' said Gobbo. 'Listen. It's humming.'

Jacob took it suspiciously and held it to his ear. It wasn't only humming like a dynamo, it was trembling too. It gave out a sense of awesome power.

'Wow,' Jacob said. 'That's pretty keen. It's going to go a long way, that banana. Now put it back in the box and – '

'Gaf!' said a voice urgently from behind him.

It was Prakash. Jacob was so startled that he dropped the banana, but Gobbo caught it before it hit the ground and stashed it in the box again.

'Where you been, man?' said Jacob hotly. 'You know what's been *happening*? What you been doing?'

'Listen,' Prakash said. He was looking desperate. 'Someone's nicked the Coolometer. The first one, I mean. And . . . It's bad, Gaf. You gotta listen carefully. Where can we go and talk?'

15

THE VORTEX

Mr Parkinson was definitely rattled. After the trouser incident, he decided he needed to consult Headquarters, so during break he borrowed the Deputy Head's office and took a powerful two-way radio out of his briefcase.

However, it wasn't his day, because no matter which waveband he tried, all he could get on the radio was some woman's throbbing voice saying:

'*He remembers the meadows of yesteryear, and gnashes his gums together to express his anguish . . .*'

Strange hollow bonking sounds came out of the speaker. Mr Parkinson turned it off in despair and looked out of the window. Ah! What was that?

The bell had just gone, and most of the kids were on their way inside, but from the Deputy Head's window Mr Parkinson could see the edge of the school kitchen. And sneaking round to the little yard where the dustbins were kept were Jacob, and Gobbo, and . . .

All of them. They were up to something. Got 'em at last! Now, if only he could get out of here without that clown of a Headmaster seeing him . . .

Mr Parkinson opened the door, looked both ways, and tiptoed carefully off towards the kitchen.

In the heart of the Cool Board, Henry was in a video-trance.

After his all-night confession, they'd given him a TV set to look at, so as to help him calm down. They'd put a stack of promotional videos on; they were designed to prepare the public for the forthcoming privatisation, and Mr Cashman thought they might as well use Henry as a guinea-pig, now they had him, to see how effective they were.

He was just watching 'Executives at Play: New Styles of Leisure Management' when the screen suddenly went BLIT, and a picture of Sandra appeared. Henry sat up, rubbing his eyes. Something had happened to the signal; that was definitely Sandra, and she seemed to be sitting in Memorial Square, clutching her poetry book. Henry goggled through the static and fiddled with the picture as he saw another figure sitting next to her.

'Yeah, I know what you mean,' this other figure was saying. 'I been disappointed too. I had me heart set on this, see, and it was dashed away from me. You can't rely on no-one.'

'Oh, that's *awful*,' Sandra said. 'I do know what you mean. I had just the same experience with Hen – with my boyfriend. I don't think he had as much depth as I hoped he did. D'you know what I mean, Alex?'

Alex?

Henry squeaked with outrage. There was no doubt about it: that was Alex, all the way down to his white socks. And Sandra was sitting there saying these appalling things … He couldn't believe it.

'I think you're a very sensitive person really, aren't you, Alex?' she went on. 'Under that cruel, devil-may-care exterior?'

'Yeah,' said Alex. 'I reckon I am. I don't think anyone's noticed that before, Sandra.'

Henry stood up.

'Nnyyaaarrggghhhh!' he said.

A dark primitive rage filled him, and he bounded to the door and with one swift kick demolished it entirely. A Security Guard picking his nose in the corridor nearly fell over with surprise. Henry swept him aside and made for the entrance.

He'd knocked out three more guards and smashed his way through the external door before Mr Cashman heard about it.

'This is the breakthrough, men!' he said. "Follow him!'

Pausing only to tell Sylvianne to contact 10 Downing Street with news of an imminent success, he shot off after Henry, who was making for Memorial Square like a cyclone.

'Right, what's going on?' said Jacob, sitting on the nearest dustbin.

'It's a catastrophe!' said Prakash. 'When I woke up this morning and saw all them giant blips on the barograph I knew it had happened. It was the bananas that gave me the clue.'

'Bananas?' said Gobbo.

'There was a bunch in our kitchen, right, and they'd all straightened out. I found out that the banana was generating a build-up of gas at the curved end, and when the – '

'Watch out,' said Deirdre.

The kitchen door opened, and Mr Parkinson's gleaming head looked out. He peered to left and right, and then saw them on the dustbins, and jumped.

'Oh! Ha, ha! Hello!' he said. 'A little informal seminar in the fresh air, eh? Jolly good!'

They stared up at him coldly.

Then he jumped again, because the cook had come up behind and tapped him forcefully on the shoulder.

'What d'you want?' she said.

'Ah! Mrs – er – the cook. I'm a – er – a Hygiene Inspector,' he said. 'Just having a look round. What's – er – what's on the menu today, Mrs Er?'

'Banana Surprise,' she said. 'And if you don't think I'm hygienic, you've got another think coming. You can inspect every knife and fork, every spoon, every – '

'No, no,' said Mr Parkinson weakly, 'that won't be necessary, Mrs Umm – '

'Oh yes it will,' she said. 'You can start with the bananas. They're through here in the larder.'

Helplessly, he vanished. Prakash looked alarmed.

'I wonder if I ought to warn them?' he said.

'Warn 'em what?' said Nings.

'Well, when the pressure inside the skin gets to the critical point, the banana bursts out of the end, and – '

There was a small explosion from the kitchen, followed by a loud SPLAT and a yell of fear.

'What did she say was on the menu?' said Julie.

'Banana Surprise,' said Deirdre. 'I reckon he's just had one.'

There was another BANG! SPLAT from the kitchen, and Jacob turned to Gobbo.

'Where's yours?' he said.

'What, my banana? In my lunch box. I left it somewhere. I better go and get it in case anyone – '

'And I was *holding* it!' Jacob said in horror. 'I held it up to my *ear*!'

The enormity of what had nearly happened took his breath away. But Prakash was impatient.

'Listen, this is *urgent*, man,' he said. 'I been at the computer ever since breakfast. What with the bananas and the radio interference and all, and the blip-co-ordinates, I think it's gone too far to turn back. We're into the vortex.'

'What's that then?' said Julie.

'All the cool in the universe,' said Prakash urgently, 'is whirling round in a great big whirlpool kind of thing, getting faster and faster. I got it tracked with the direction-finder on the new Coolometer. It's poised right above Memorial Square. And we got about an hour and – ' he looked at his watch – 'and five minutes before it strikes.'

'Strikes? What d'you mean, strikes?' said Jacob.

'Like lightning,' said Prakash. 'Like you have a lightning-rod, right, to attract the electricity in the clouds. Well, this vortex is building up a massive cool charge, and as soon as the right person comes along, it's gonna go FZAP and coolify 'em.'

There was silence among the dustbins as this sank in.

Then Deirdre said, 'But what d'you mean by the right sort of person? Someone cool?'

'No, no. Not at all. Just the opposite, like magnets, to attract it. It's gotta be someone well thick. Someone really solid, right, someone who'd never be cool in a million years. Course, afterwards, they'd be the coolest person in the world, no question. If they survived.'

There was another silence.

'You mean – ' said Nings.

'Yeah,' said Prakash.

'You mean we could lose *everything*?' said Jacob.

'Yeah. Unless we find the right sort of person and peg 'em out in Memorial Square as soon as possible.'

'Who can we get?' said Jacob, feeling the panic rise. 'Whoever's in charge after the vortex hits will clean up, man! They'll rule the cool!'

Desperately, they thought of all their friends, all the wimps, all the morons . . . Then all at once they knew.

'Mr Staines,' said Jacob and Deirdre simultaneously.

And they shot away to look for him like a bunch of straight bananas.

Mr Staines had been having an uncomfortable time over the last half-hour or so.

To start with, he was in the secretary's office when some teacher came in and started going on and on about

172

the minibus.

'I *booked it out*!' he said. 'I wrote my name in the diary! I checked the logbook! I did everything I should have done, and where is it? Where's it gone? Who's got it?'

'Well, there was an entirely unforeseen – '

'There was nothing unforeseen about my trip to the Museum – it's been foreseen for weeks! Looks, there it is on the calendar! We've booked a speaker! *Where's the minibus*?'

Mr Staines spread his hands helplessly.

'What can I say?' he said. 'This is a school. These things happen.'

'Well, you're supposed to stop them happening, aren't you?'

'Well, yes and no; but on the other hand – '

'Who's got it? Where is it? What's this unforeseen rubbish that's more important than a planned, authorised, notified, booked, official visit to the Museum, with a visiting speaker from the University? Eh?'

'Oh, now, come on, Lew, there are valuable things going on apart from your visits, you know. Let a hundred flowers bloom!'

'But I *booked* it – '

Just then a little girl came up and plucked at Mr Staines's sleeve. He'd told the kids many times that he was always available, and he'd never turn them away, so they kept wandering up to him at all hours, wherever he was.

He held up his hand to stop the teacher in mid-flow.

'Now hang on,' he said. 'First things first. What is it, lovey?'

'I found this,' said the weenie, holding out Gobbo's lunch box.

'Oh, someone's lost their dinner, have they?' said Mr Staines. 'That's very good of you to bring it to me.

173

We'll give you a merit mark for that. They'd've worried, wouldn't they, eh? I wonder whose it is?'

The teacher threw up his hands and left. Mr Staines shook his head sadly as he opened the lunch-box.

'D'you know, Mary,' he said to Mrs Blanchard, 'I think there are some members of this staff who don't actually like children. Well, I'm blowed – look at this! A straight banaaaAAGGHH – '

Five minutes later, when she'd got him cleaned up, he realised it was time for the Mermaid Club, and toddled off to get changed.

The Mermaid Club was what he called his group of non-swimmers from the First Year. The younger the kids were and the less they could do, the more he liked them, and he was really at home with this bunch. It was the high point of his week. He took them in the school swimming pool and they'd all splash about together getting familiar with the water.

When Jacob and Deirdre arrived at his office, he'd already left. Mrs Blanchard looked at them suspiciously.

'What d'you want Mr Staines for?'

'It's that visitor,' said Deirdre. 'He asked if we could find him. It's urgent, honestly.'

'Well, he's in the swimming pool with the Mermaid Club. And d'you know anything about this?'

She held out Gobbo's lunch box.

'No,' said Jacob innocently.

'H'mm,' she said.

They belted out to the swimming pool while the others waited with their bikes in the car park out of sight. They could hear the yelling and splashing through the fence, but they weren't prepared for the sight that met them when they got inside.

Mr Staines was charging up and down the shallow

end, wearing a pink rubber hat and a huge swimming costume made out of what looked like some kind of dietary fibre. There were squealing weenies clinging to his legs and climbing on his shoulders, and he had a small girl tucked under each arm, and he was going 'Brrroom brrroom brroom! Wheeee!'

He stopped dead when he saw Jacob and Deirdre. Half the weenies fell off, and a tidal wave surged up and broke over the edge of the pool.

'Hello!' he called. 'You looking for me?'

Deirdre recovered her voice before Jacob did, and said shakily 'Yeah. This is an emergency, Mr Staines. We – er – we – er – '

'We got to get to Memorial Square,' Jacob put in. 'And you gotta come, and all. It's – er – we – '

'The Duke of Edinburgh's Award!' said Deirdre.

'Yeah, that's it!' said Jacob. 'An initiative test. We gotta find a Head Teacher and get him to Memorial Square by quarter past twelve, and we'll qualify for an award. There's going to be photographers from the paper there, and all.'

'Oh, really?' said Mr Staines. 'Well be in the newspapers! How about that, mermaids!'

He dumped his little girls and surged out of the water. Jacob hooked out a couple of weenies who were drowning and draped them over the edge while Mr Staines rubbed himself dry.

'In you go, now, mermaids!' he told them. 'Tell Mrs Blanchard I've had to go out. It's lunch time now anyway – she can manage on her own. You run round to the car park,' he said to Jacob and Deirdre. 'We'll go in my car. This is a big day, eh!'

Two minutes later he came waddling round the corner. He was so excited he hadn't bothered to change; he was still wearing his dietary-fibre trunks, but he'd put on grey nylon socks and lace-up shoes, and a big T-shirt saying 'Smile! The world loves you'.

As he started the car and leaned over to open the passenger door, Jacob said to Deirdre, 'How can we lose?'

'Don't speak too soon,' she muttered. 'Anything could happen yet.'

Mr Parkinson, still trembling from the banana-strike, belted round the corner into Memorial Square. Despite receiving two good ones in the face, he'd managed to stagger close enough to the window to overhear what Prakash had been saying, and he thought his only chance was to make for the Square and get in first.

When he saw Mr Cashman hurrying into the Square too, he nearly cried with relief. He ran up and shook him by the shoulder.

'What the devil's the matter with you, Parkinson?' Mr Cashman snarled. 'Look at the mess you're in.'

'Listen!' panted Mr Parkinson, and told him quickly about the vortex.

'So,' said Mr Cashman. 'That was their secret weapon. How long have we got?'

'It could strike at any moment,' said Mr Parkinson. 'We've just got to find someone uncool. Put 'em under contract and peg 'em out and hope for the best. What about your escaped prisoner?'

Mr Cashman glanced over at Henry, who'd reached the bench where Sandra and Alex were having their conversation. As they watched, Henry picked Alex up with one hand and shook him like a rattle. Sandra screeched, and Henry dropped Alex and swept Sandra into his arms.

'No,' said Mr Cashman. 'He's too cool now. Wait a minute! What in the world is that?'

He was looking at the centre of the square, where a mob of excited-looking kids were all banging tambourines and singing. Mr Cashman rubbed his eyes.

'I believe we've got it,' he said. 'Quick! Follow me!'

He leapt up the steps, and shoved aside a bunch of curious spectators so he could get a clearer view. It was a remarkable sight. Two small kids in a donkey costume were lying on the ground with their legs in the air, while the other kids were singing 'Ohhh – ohhh – ohhh ... '

Then a fat woman with a red face came dancing in and yelled encouragingly 'The Donkey Dental Hospital is only a mile away, Derek! Take courage, for this is Herefordshire!'

'Mmmpf nnmmpf mmmphf,' mumbled the donkey.

'Only the kiss of life can restore him now!' cried the old girl, and bent over. The weenies' chorus rose to a throbbing climax as she fastened her mouth to the donkey's tormented lips.

Mr Cashman summed her up at once. He stepped forward and tapped her on the shoulder.

'Excuse me, madam,' he said smoothly. 'I wonder if I could have a word? I'm from the Arts Council ... '

Memorial Square was seething with weirdness. As well as the wild inhabitants and the swarms of policemen, there were all kinds of strange things going on, as Jacob and Deirdre saw when they dragged Mr Staines out of his car and on to the grass.

There was a peaceful-looking bunch of Detrendifiers watching *Bonanza* on the old Coolometer; there was Prakash's new direction-finding model pointed upright nearby, with Prakash checking the screen; there were two dusty-looking blokes having a fight by a bench, while Sandra sat next to them writing a poem about it; there was a burial service going on for a dead donkey; there were Nings and Gobbo and Julie and David flinging their bikes down and belting up the steps ...

'Tie him up!' yelled Jacob to the others.

Deirdre started to tie Mr Staines to the nearest tree with the tow-rope from his car. Half a dozen punks were watching in a thoughtful kind of way, as if they were working out the range and wondering what to throw. Mr Staines didn't much like the look of them.

'Is this going to take long, Debbie?' he said.

Deirdre looked up. Somewhere above them the *vortex* was spinning faster and faster.

'I shouldn't worry,' Deirdre told him. 'You'll be feeling pretty cool in a couple of minutes.'

Then she noticed that Jacob was staring across the square.

'Here,' he said. 'Look ... '

He pointed to Mr Cashman, who was doing something strange beside the drinking fountain. It wasn't as strange as what most of the inhabitants did in it, but it was pretty odd all the same. He was handcuffing a crazy-looking woman to it, and she was yelling 'Improvise! Improvise!' at the donkey's funeral party.

Jacob and Deirdre shot across to have a closer look, and Mr Cashman glanced up and saw them.

'Ha, ha!' he said. 'Too late!'

'That's what you think,' said Jacob. 'Look what we got.'

Mr Cashman looked across at Mr Staines, and recoiled in amazement.

'Good grief,' he said. 'How did you find *him*?'

'Duke of Edinburgh's Award,' said Jacob. 'How'd you get this old girl?'

'Arts Council.'

'Oh,' said Jacob. 'Smart.'

'Ours'll win,' said Deirdre.

'D'you want to buy him?' said Jacob. 'I mean, look at him. Your old girl's nowhere.'

Mr Cashman snarled. 'How much?' he said.

But then there came a yell from Prakash. He pointed up at the sky, and a huge kind of rushing sound filled the air. Everyone looked up.

'It's the VORTEX!' shouted Mr Parkinson. 'It's enormous – terrifying – '

It was like standing in the plughole of a colossal bath. The cool was whizzing round faster and faster, and then with an almighty

– the *vortex* struck.

16

AFTER THE VORTEX

Silence.

Nothing happened. Everything was still.

Mr Staines was still tied to his tree, Pippa from The Big Pixie still handcuffed to the drinking fountain, and they both looked as terrible as ever.

It hadn't worked ...

Jacob and Mr Cashman looked at each other, wide-eyed. Where had it gone? What had happened to all that cool? Somehow, in about a third of a second, it had passed out of their control for good.

And then there was a gasp of wonder from across the Square. A cry of admiration – applause – cheers – as a Vision drifted out of the shopping precinct. Jacob's hand found Deirdre's and clutched it in sheer terror.

'I don't believe it,' he whispered, as the traffic parted and kids ran forward for autographs and an old guy selling flowers grabbed an armful and flung them down in front of her.

For the Vision was Louise.

Somehow, everything about her was fascinating. The charming little wisps of dust in her hair – the bold, provocative orange of her top lip, and the shy, delicate white of her lower one – the rosy little spots clustered timidly on her chin – the thrilling contrast between the fragrant pyjamas, with their witty motif in cocoa, and the neo-brutalism of the tattered rain-coat – and the

hypnotic movement of her jaw ... And the ...
And ...

She was *it*. The vortex had struck all right. She was the coolest thing in the universe.

Jacob pulled himself together. Was that David there, kneeling down and worshipping? And Nings? And –

'Come *on*,' Deirdre was saying. 'Else he'll sign her up for good.'

'Eh? Blimey – '

There was a throng all round her, with flash-bulbs and cameras and microphones appearing from nowhere. And in the middle of it all, holding a cheque-book, talking fast, was Mr Cashman.

Jacob and Deirdre zoomed across at once.

'Here!' he said. 'Get lost. She's my sister.'

'Fancy that,' said Mr Cashman. 'And now she's my client. Goodbye.'

'Oh, no, she ain't. I got first claim. Anyway, what you offering? Ten per cent? Listen, Louise – '

'No, listen to *me*,' said Mr Cashman, elbowing him aside. 'Louise! What a pretty name! I can see it now – the cover of *Vogue* – the videos – the fame – '

'Don't listen to him,' said Jacob urgently, shoving in front again. 'He's a creep. He'll rip you off as soon as look at you. You need a manager – '

Then the Vision spoke.

'Get lost,' she said.

Wow! everyone thought. Witty as well as beautiful! Amazing.

'Yes,' said Mr Cashman, recovering quickly from the dazzling cool-beams. 'Go away, Jacob. This is a job for grown-ups. Come with me, my dear ... '

'And you push off and all,' she said.

Another ripple of wonder went round the stunned spectators. What a gift for language!

'No, *listen*,' Jacob said, 'you don't realise what's

happened. You can't just – '

'It's no good, Gaf,' Deirdre said. 'Look.'

For the crowd was parting.

And into Memorial Square rode the pride of the city's police force, the Mounted Escort Division, their tricycles twinkling red and blue and green in the sunshine; and behind them came a huge car – a car with little flags fluttering on the wings – a car with a young man in a suit sitting in the back . . .

The car drew up. The chauffeur got out, lifted his cap, and said something quietly to Louise.

The crowd was agog. Was it? It couldn't be – it wasn't, surely –

Louise stared at the chauffeur, and then slowly took out her bubble gum and dropped it in the gutter.

'Yeah,' she said. 'All right.'

She got in, and the chauffeur saluted. As the car pulled away, several old ladies got out Union Jacks and cried 'Gawd bless her!'

There was a scramble for her discarded bubble gum. David got there first. He cut it into twenty-six little bits with his Swiss Army knife and started selling them for 50p each.

Just then, Prakash came belting up.

'We're safe!' he said. 'The blips are finished. The universe is back in order. Who copped the vortex, then?'

'My sister,' said Jacob. 'All that effort, and my whale of a sister ends up with all the cool. Seems to me there's no justice in the world.'

'How right you are,' said a sorrowful voice behind him.

Jacob turned to see Mr Cashman.

'What d'you want?' he said.

'Have you got a moment?' said Mr Cashman, drawing him aside into the entrance of the sports shop, where they wouldn't be overheard. 'It looks as if we've reached a stalemate. You can't go forward – *we* can't go forward. But despite this little temporary setback, we've got great plans, big opportunities, a golden future. And I've been very impressed by your organization. It's dynamic, it's creative, it's got flair and vision. Why not join forces? Separately, we're done for. Together, we can – '

'How much?'

'I'm talking share options, I'm talking seats on the Board, I'm talking six-figure sweeteners – '

Jacob felt his eyeballs bulging. With an effort, he sucked them in again. This sounded pretty good. He looked around furtively – and saw Julie, Prakash, David, Nings, Gobbo, and Deirdre all frowning at him two feet away. He gulped, and looked back sternly at Mr Cashman.

'You're panicking,' he said.

'No! I'm not!' said Mr Cashman, mopping his forehead. 'I'm just – '

'Well, the answer's no,' said Jacob.

'You'll regret it! I warn you! I won't make this offer twice! You'll suffer for this! I warn you!'

'Yeah, yeah,' said Deirdre.

'Right, you've done it now,' said Mr Cashman. 'You've asked for it. Parkinson!' he shouted, scuttling away. 'Parkinson! My car, quickly!' And he yelled back over his shoulder, 'You'll regret this as long as you – '

Shouting backwards and running forwards, he didn't see the lamppost, and he ran into it with a colossal BONG! before sliding to the ground, stunned.

'H'mm,' said Jacob, wondering what a six-figure sweetener was. Something to do with food, probably. 'Here,' he said to David, 'how much did you get for that bubble gum?'

'Thirteen quid,' said David.

'Well, go and get us some hamburgers then. I'm starving.'

'What we gonna do about ... ' said Gobbo, and waved his hand vaguely to indicate *everything*.

Jacob thought of Mr Staines, tied to his tree, with the wild natives of the Square closing in. He thought of the lessons they'd bunked off from. He thought of the French homework he hadn't done. He thought of Mr Cashman's threats. He thought of Louise.

'Do?' he said. 'What we always do. We're just gonna stay cool.'